R0110685583

12/2018

THE GRAY HUNTER'S REVENGE

READ ALL THE MYSTERIES IN THE
HARDY BOYS ADVENTURES:

HARDY BOYS ADVENTURES™

#17 THE GRAY HUNTER'S REVENGE

FRANKLIN W. DIXON

ALADDIN   New York London Toronto Sydney New Delhi

ALADDIN

An imprint of Simon & Schuster Children's Publishing Division
1230 Avenue of the Americas, New York, NY 10020
First Aladdin hardcover edition October 2018
Text copyright © 2018 by Simon & Schuster, Inc.
Cover illustration copyright © 2018 by Kevin Keele
THE HARDY BOYS MYSTERY SERIES, HARDY BOYS ADVENTURES,
and related logos are trademarks of Simon & Schuster, Inc.
Also available in an Aladdin paperback edition.

For information about special discounts for bulk purchases, please contact Simon & Schuster
Special Sales at 1-866-506-1949 or business@simonandschuster.com.
The Simon & Schuster Speakers Bureau can bring authors to your live event.
For more information or to book an event contact the Simon & Schuster Speakers Bureau
at 1-866-248-3049 or visit our website at www.simonspeakers.com.
Series designed by Karin Paprocki
Interior designed by Mike Rosamilia
The text of this book was set in Adobe Caslon Pro.
Manufactured in the United States of America 0918 FFG
2 4 6 8 10 9 7 5 3 1
Library of Congress Cataloging-in-Publication Data
Names: Dixon, Franklin W., author. | Title: The gray hunter's revenge / Franklin W. Dixon.
Description: First Aladdin hardcover/paperback edition. | New York : Aladdin, 2018. |
Series: Hardy Boys adventures ; #17 | Summary: The Hardy Boys are asked to investigate
when their favorite thriller writer dies in what may have been an accident, while the press
swarms Bayport to get information about the author's last novel.
Identifiers: LCCN 2017061138 (print) | LCCN 2018006771 (eBook) |
ISBN 9781534411524 (eBook) | ISBN 9781534411500 (pbk) | ISBN 9781534411517 (hc)
Subjects: | CYAC: Authors—Fiction. | Death—Fiction. | Haunted houses—Fiction. |
Brothers—Fiction. | Mystery and detective stories. | BISAC: JUVENILE FICTION /
Mysteries & Detective Stories. | JUVENILE FICTION / Action & Adventure / General.
Classification: LCC PZ7.D644 (eBook) | LCC PZ7.D644 Gp 2018 (print) |
DDC [Fic]—dc23
LC record available at https://lccn.loc.gov/2017061138

CONTENTS

HOUSE OF HORRORS

1

JOE

THE HOUSE STOOD HIGH ON A HILL, surrounded by the skeletons of trees. Dozens of crows perched on the trees' branches, filling the silence with their harsh squawking. Frank and I stood next to the car, where he'd parked it after driving through the tall, wrought-iron gates. Gates that had been kept closed for as long as anyone can remember. Closed and locked, until today.

As an amateur detective, I've been up against some crazy stuff in my time. Ruthless criminals. Fiery explosions. Killer sharks—to name a few. But Cliffside Manor was a whole new level of terrifying. I mean, sure, it was just a house. But the things that had supposedly happened inside that house, well . . . They were things that would keep even the bravest soul up at night.

I couldn't *wait* to get inside!

"You ready?" Frank asked, a chill, late-autumn breeze ruffling his dark brown hair.

I zipped my coat against the cold and glanced back up at the house. It was constructed of stone bricks that were almost black with age, and it sported a chimney on each side—one of them crumbling. Two large bay windows looked out across the estate like unblinking eyes, dark and forbidding. "I was born ready," I replied with a grin.

We started to walk toward the house, passing a dozen other parked cars on the way. "Looks like we're not the only ones coming to the estate sale," Frank observed.

I snorted. "Are you kidding me? I'm surprised the entire county isn't here. Who in their right mind would pass up the chance to go inside the hundred-year-old, super-scary, super-haunted house?"

"Not Joe Hardy," Frank muttered, smirking.

"Darn right, not Joe Hardy!" I said. "Not only that, I might get to buy something belonging to one of the greatest horror writers of all time—Nathan Foxwood!"

Frank's smile fell. "It's awful about the car accident," he said. "I know you really liked his books."

"Yeah," I replied, kicking a rock across the long driveway. "I did." Nathan Foxwood's books weren't as popular now, but back in the day, he was one of the most famous authors in the world. A handful of his books had even been made into movies. When I was little, there was always a tattered Nathan Foxwood paperback on my dad's nightstand—usually with some kind of scary picture on the front, and a portrait of the author himself on the back. He was a wolfish-looking guy—with dark hair and a short beard, and piercing eyes that seemed to bore right into you. Once I found out I was supposedly too young to read them, I promptly "borrowed" one from Dad's bedroom and hid in the closet to binge-read it with a flashlight. From then on, I was hooked.

A few years ago, the news spread that Mr. Foxwood and his wife were buying the abandoned estate on the outskirts of town—the infamous Cliffside Manor. No one could understand why he'd want to live in such a terrible place—but I could. Nathan Foxwood's books were always full of the scariest things imaginable, so I figured maybe he was just trying to get some new material firsthand. I had always hoped to run into him in downtown Bayport and get to meet one of my idols, but it never happened.

And now, it was too late.

Just three days ago, sometime in the middle of the night, Mr. Foxwood came tearing down the hill from the manor in his car, lost control, and careened right off the side of the cliff that bordered the estate. The car burned at the bottom of the ravine for hours before anyone found out.

Rumors had been swirling ever since that Mr. Foxwood had been working on a new novel since he'd moved into town—a book about Cliffside Manor itself, and its dark history. If that were true, it was a shame that he'd never get to finish it. I'd been waiting years for a new Nathan Foxwood novel!

"Still," Frank said with a wary look around the place. "I'm not entirely sure this is a good idea. The last time you and I got close to something belonging to one of our favorite authors, we got framed for theft."

"Oh," I said, my shoulders slumping. "That." Frank was talking about when he and I got caught up in a bad situation with an old adversary who had it in for us. We had gone to check out an original copy of one of Sir Arthur Conan Doyle's Sherlock Holmes manuscripts at the Bayport Museum and noticed that there were some pages missing. Imagine our surprise when those missing pages started turning up in our car and lockers at school! Things were pretty hairy for a while, but thankfully, it was all right in the end, and our names were cleared of any wrongdoing.

"Look, Frank," I continued. "I know that was bad, but the whole mess is behind us now! C'mon, don't ruin this with your worrying. Nothing bad is going to happen at Cliffside Manor!"

In the next moment, a strong breeze swept through the trees, causing a large acorn to come plummeting down from above and plonk Frank right on the top of the head.

"Yow!" he said, wincing. He rubbed the spot and sighed. "'Nothing bad,' eh? Famous last words."

As Frank and I approached the house, we saw a large group of people milling around near the front entrance. "Is that a reporter?" Frank asked, eyeballing a woman on the edge of the crowd holding a notepad and a camera bag. She was tall, with deep brown skin, and had twists of black hair cascading down her back.

"Might be," I said.

"Well, try to control yourself this time, will you?"

I rolled my eyes. I flirt with *one reporter* who then goes and gets us in trouble with the police, and now I'll never hear the end of it. As we reached the crowd, the wind picked up suddenly, and I watched as the reporter's notepad went flying out of her hands and landed at my feet.

I picked up the notepad and threw a backward glance at Frank, and shrugged. "I was totally planning on controlling myself, bro," I said. "But it looks like the universe has other ideas." I strolled over to the young woman and handed back the notepad.

"Thanks," she said with a wide smile. "Seems like the weather is conspiring to be as creepy as this house."

"Totally," I agreed. "Are you here to cover the estate sale?"

She nodded. "Aisha Best. I'm a reporter with the *Bayport Bugle*. I'm actually hoping to snag an interview with Heather Foxwood—the writer's wife. I've heard that she's got quite the story about what went on in there before her husband died. No one's been able to get ahold of her since the accident, so I'm trying to get an exclusive." Aisha quirked her head at me. "What brings you here to the sale, Mr. . . . ?"

I sneaked a look back at Frank, who was standing a few feet away with his arms crossed, looking less than thrilled. "Umm," I said, biting my lip. "Oh, I'm just a fan, that's all. Looking to pick up some memorabilia."

Aisha raised an eyebrow and looked like she was about to ask more questions, when the front door of the manor opened. Everyone in the crowd went quiet instantly.

A wiry guy with a shaved head and copper-colored skin poked his head out of the door, his eyes roving the scene through black-rimmed glasses. He was also wearing a bow tie that seemed to be decorated with other tiny bow ties—which I thought was a little weird, but hey, it's fashion, who am I to talk? After checking his wristwatch and adjusting the bow tie, he stepped out of the house and opened his arms in welcome.

"Hello, everyone," he said loudly, "and thank you for coming to the estate sale here at Cliffside Manor. My name is Adam Parker, and I'm the late Mr. Foxwood's assistant. I'm sure you're all eager to come in out of the cold, so please step inside the house and I'll explain how all this works."

Frank and I filed in behind the rest of the crowd as they trooped though the front door. I elbowed my brother in excitement as we climbed up the stone stairs at the entry-way. "We're going in! Hardly anyone has been inside this place in decades!"

Frank nodded, his eyes flashing with curiosity. "The place is probably like a time capsule. There might be boxes of hundred-year-old newspapers just sitting around in a basement somewhere!"

I snorted. "Bro, need I remind you that we are about to enter *Cliffside Manor*? As in, the most haunted house on this side of the Mississippi? And you're revving your engines over some pile of dusty newspapers?"

"Hey," Frank retorted. "At least newspapers are *real*. What do you expect, for some phantasm to come sailing through the walls and take a selfie with you?"

"No," I said, annoyed. Of course, when he said it that way, being so excited about the haunted aspect of the manor did seem a little silly. "Anyway," I continued as we crossed the threshold into the house, "ghosts or no ghosts, you've got to admit—this house has seen its share of sinister stuff."

Frank nodded, and I saw his eyes flick around nervously as we stepped into the front room. Legend had it that the people who'd first owned the house, a wealthy, aristocratic family, had unknowingly built it on a piece of land belonging to a solitary man who lived in a cabin in the woods nearby. The man, who hunted deer and rabbits for food, was furious that this family had taken over and spoiled his land, but he had no legal leg to stand on and therefore wasn't taken seriously by the family or anyone in town. The story goes that one particular night, when a raucous dinner party filled the forest with noise and light all night, the man broke into the house carrying an ax—and left no one inside alive. Once the horrific scene was discovered, the local police pursued him into the dark forest, where he supposedly threw himself over the cliff's edge. His body was never found.

No one wanted to live in the manor after that. Gossip hung around the place like a cloud of smoke—people claimed to see the figure of the man, who they named the Gray Hunter, lurking in the shadows of the house, frightening off anyone who dared to enter. Of course, plenty of people think the whole story was nothing more than an urban legend meant to be told around a campfire, but still—just looking at the house gave you the willies.

As we entered the foyer, what I found there did nothing to dispel the idea that the place was, like, *100 percent* haunted. Heavy velvet curtains covered every window, and the only light that pierced the gloom came from a dusty chandelier above our heads. Where there weren't creepy oil paintings of little girls and long-dead rich guys in old-fashioned clothing, the walls were covered in peeling, olive-colored wallpaper. The whole place smelled of mold, overlaid with a cloying vanilla scent that must have been sprayed around in an attempt to mask the stench of rot. It was quiet except for the ticking of a hulking grandfather clock and the wind moaning through the rafters, a sound that sent shivers down my spine.

It. Was. Awesome!

I glanced over at Frank to see if he was enjoying this as

much as I was. "Isn't this great?" I asked him. "It's so creepy! I can totally imagine a Nathan Foxwood book about this place."

"The atmosphere is pretty cool," Frank admitted, studying the room. But then he wrinkled his nose. "I could do without the smell, though."

The guy called Adam had climbed halfway up the staircase to the second floor and was trying to get everyone's attention. "Welcome to Cliffside Manor," he said over the murmuring of the crowd. "All the items for sale by the Foxwood estate are clearly marked with labels and suggested prices. If you are interested in purchasing an item, simply pick it up and bring it down to this room to complete the sale." He gestured toward a table where several people sat with open laptops and a cash box. "If an item is too large to lift, you can ask one of the assistants here to mark it sold on your behalf. Please be courteous to other customers—there are a lot of you here today, and I realize that people can sometimes get a little carried away at these events. Just remember, an armoire is not worth a broken arm." Adam waggled his eyebrows and paused as some of the guests tittered.

"Ugh," said Frank. "Puns."

"And finally . . ." Adam's voice trailed off. He looked unsure of what to say next, but finally cleared his throat and continued. "Just be careful. As you all probably know, this is a very old house, and things can happen unexpectedly in places like these." He clapped his hands once, as if trying to clear the air of mystery that surrounded his words. "Well! I won't take up any more of your time. Good hunting, everyone!"

That Adam guy wasn't kidding about people getting carried away! The moment he stopped talking, people in the crowd immediately shot off in different directions, all of them vying to get to the most valuable items before anyone else could. "Well," said Frank, "I'm not really interested in getting into a fistfight over a writing desk, but I would like to pick up a few books. So I'm going to check out the study. I heard that Nathan Foxwood had a ton of true-crime books in his collection—I'd like to snag a few if they aren't too expensive. Where are you off to?"

I rubbed my hands together in anticipation. "I'd like to buy something if I can, but I want to do a little exploring first. Get away from the crowd and take it all in. How often do you get to just walk around a place like this?"

Frank nodded and said he'd meet back up with me in the main room in half an hour. With most of the shoppers milling around the first floor, I thought I'd get away from the pack and head upstairs. I loped up the steps two at a time until I reached the landing, where two murky hallways led away from the balcony that looked down on the foyer below. So I did what I always did when I faced a choice like this—I turned left.

The second floor of the house was no less creepy than the first—and being alone up there only increased the freaky factor tenfold. Everything was covered with a thick layer of dust, and cobwebs lurked invisibly in the air, only to be discovered by my face when I walked straight into one.

After recovering from that unpleasant, creepy-crawly sensation, I have to admit—I was starting to get a little freaked out. I kept getting this weird feeling that someone was watching me, but whenever I turned around, there was no one there.

Get ahold of yourself, Hardy! I thought. I mean, wasn't this what I wanted? A real-life haunted house experience? For all I knew, Nathan Foxwood himself had walked down these halls, getting inspiration for whatever he'd been working on before he died. *I wonder if this place freaked him out too.*

As if in answer, somewhere up ahead there was an ear-splitting scream.

THE HUNT BEGINS

2

FRANK

WHILE JOE WENT OFF IN SEARCH of poltergeists upstairs, I decided to check out Nathan Foxwood's study. By the time I got there, it looked like a lot of the hot-ticket items had already been snatched up and the crowd had moved on—I found myself alone in the room. It had had a high ceiling and wall-to-wall bookshelves—many of them now half-empty after being pillaged by the shoppers. Even the great mahogany desk near the window already had a SOLD sticker on it!

"Man," I said to myself. "These people don't play around!"

I was surprised to see that the antique black typewriter on the desk hadn't been taken as well, but then again, it didn't have a tag, so maybe it wasn't for sale. I remembered reading in Nathan Foxwood's obituary that he was infamously old-fashioned when it came to his writing—he apparently never used a computer, preferring to write his books on typewriters.

I noticed a piece of paper was still set inside the typewriter, with half a page of writing left incomplete midsentence. It was a little spooky, seeing it left behind like that, knowing that the man who had been working away at it would never get to finish the thought. I leaned over to read the words on the page, my curiosity getting the best of me.

The night was full of creeping shadows, I read, *and my heart leaped, sickeningly, at each creak of the house, at every moan across the gutters. I felt like a deer in the woods, smelling the hunter on the breath of the wind, knowing that though I still lived my fate was sealed. And then I saw him. Too large to be a living man, and too silent besides—he appeared like a devil at my bedroom door, lit from within by an unearthly glow and hefting an ax in his hands. "The Hunter," I whispered. I had scoffed at the villagers' warnings, ignored their dread tales—but I had been wrong. I hadn't believed in the Hunter, but he did not need my belief to come for my blood. I opened my mouth to*

That was all.

Having never really been interested in horror stories myself, I'd never picked one up, though Joe pushed them in my face as often as he could. But reading this now, I could see why he liked them. The words sort of grabbed you and didn't let go. Despite myself, I shivered.

And then, I felt a prickle at my neck. A sensation like I was being watched. Figuring it was just another shopper who had come into the room while I was reading, I turned around to face them—but there was no one there. And then movement outside the window caught my eye, and I looked through the gauzy, threadbare curtains to see what appeared to be a figure looming on the other side. It was a large, dark shape, made featureless by the gray light behind it. I took a step closer and saw the outline of an object it seemed to be holding in its hands. A familiar object, one that glinted sharply as it moved.

An ax.

My breath caught in my throat as I stumbled back—and at that exact moment I heard the sound of a distant scream. I instinctively turned toward the sound. Had it come from upstairs? What was going on? Remembering what I'd seen, I turned back to the window, back to the dark figure—but when I looked again, it was gone.

Had I been imagining things? *Joe and his ridiculous stories are getting into my head!* I went to the window and pulled aside the thin curtains. Out on the balcony there was a decorative stone statue of a man—could that have been what I'd seen? Was it just a trick of the light?

That didn't matter now. Forcing myself to focus, I ran out of the room to try and find the source of the scream. Everyone in the front room was pointing upstairs, looking spooked, so I took two stairs at a time until I reached the landing.

"Joe!" I called out. "Where are you?"

"In here!" came his reply, from a room at the end of the hall.

I entered the murky sitting room to find Joe kneeling down next to a woman who held one shaky hand to her head, her face ashen. She looked to be in her forties, with dark, wavy hair streaked with silver, and blue eyes that fixed on me as I came in. "I heard a scream," I said, breathless. "Is everything all right?"

"Frank," Joe began, "this is Heather Foxwood." I could tell that he was trying to remain calm and serious, but there was a weird kind of excitement in his voice. And no wonder—this was his favorite author's wife! "She'd passed out when I came into the room, but she seems fine now."

"Should I call an ambulance?" I asked her.

"N-no," she managed. "I'm not ill. It's just that . . . well, I *saw* something."

"What?" I asked.

Mrs. Foxwood looked down at the floor, shaking her head. "It's impossible," she muttered to herself. "It can't be."

"Please," I urged, shooting daggers at Joe, who looked even more excited than before at this development. "Just tell us what you saw."

Mrs. Foxwood took a deep, shuddering breath before saying, "It was him. The man from the stories. The Gray Hunter."

There was a moment of silence as Joe and I let this sink

in. What was she saying? That she'd seen a ghost? There had to be another explanation. Was someone playing a cruel prank on a mourning widow?

"Tell us exactly what happened," Joe encouraged her.

"I was just in here putting tickets on a few final items," she said, "when the room suddenly got colder. And then I sensed movement out of the corner of my eye—and there he was. He appeared out of nowhere, just there"—she pointed at the stone fireplace in front of us—"with an ax in his hands. He was coming toward me, soundless, when I screamed. I must have blacked out then. When I came to, though, no one was here but this young man." She gestured at Joe, who was clearly enthralled by her story.

And so I felt it was my duty to be the voice of reason in all of this.

"Mrs. Foxwood," I said, "my name is Frank Hardy, and you've already met my brother, Joe. Solving mysteries is kind of a hobby of ours, so we've seen a lot of strange stuff—but most things turn out to have a logical explanation. Can you think of anyone who'd want to scare you like this? You are a local celebrity, and with what's happened, your name has been in the papers a lot over the past few days."

Mrs. Foxwood sighed. "I know what you're thinking— the grieving widow of a horror writer seeing ghosts in her house. It's almost cliché. But I am a *scientist*, Mr. Hardy. I don't have my head in the clouds like my husband did. I believe in *facts*. I believe in what I can see right in front of my eyes." She wrapped her arms around her shoulders as a shiver shook her. "And what I saw was something I cannot explain."

At that moment, a bunch of people—including Adam Parker—came into the room, swarming around Heather Foxwood like buzzing bees. I pulled Joe out into the hallway, trying to get away from the chaos, but even out there people were hanging around, gossiping.

"Did you hear?" one woman was saying. "Heather Foxwood saw the Hunter!"

"Really!" said an older man with her. "I just overheard a couple other folks saying they'd seen some kind of shadowy figure lurking around as they were shopping. Looks like this place is haunted after all!"

Joe was overjoyed. "It's like being in a real Nathan Foxwood novel!" he crowed.

I rolled my eyes. "You don't really think she saw a ghost, do you? It was probably just a misunderstanding. Or someone just trying to scare her—though I can't imagine why." But then I suddenly remembered what I'd seen back in the study, and I felt the blood drain from my face.

Joe noticed the change in my mood immediately. "What? What's wrong?"

I shook my head. "Nothing, nothing," I said.

But my brother's like a bloodhound—once he's picked up a scent, he'll follow it to the ends of the earth. He squinted at me and exclaimed, "You saw something too,

Adam straightened his bow tie and launched into his story. "So, being an aspiring writer myself, getting to be Nathan Foxwood's assistant seemed like a dream come true. I could learn from the best, right? And for a while, it was like that. Mr. Foxwood was a great guy—he was always full of ideas. Until recently. That's when things started to fall apart. It was almost like Mr. Foxwood was losing touch with reality. I'd find him talking to himself, claiming to see things that weren't there. He heard voices. Eventually it got bad enough that on the night of the accident, Mrs. Foxwood was so upset about his behavior that she left to go stay with a friend for the night. I tried to talk some sense into him, but Mr. Foxwood was out of his mind. He threw me out." Adam looked at the floor. "I didn't find out about the accident until late the next day. I was in shock. Anyway, I figured that was the end of it, but then all these strange things started happening. Weird noises. Whispers. Things going missing from the house. I started to think I was losing my mind too! And now all this mess at the estate sale—the reporters are already having a field day!" Adam covered his face and sighed. "Look, guys, I don't believe in ghosts any more than the next person. But something *is* going on here. Mrs. Foxwood doesn't want the police involved—she's been through enough as it is—but I need to get to the bottom of this. For Mr. Foxwood's sake. I owe him that. Would you be willing to look into it for me? I don't know where else to turn."

I had to admit, the whole situation had really piqued my interest. Even if Adam hadn't asked us to take the case, not knowing the truth about what was really going on would have nagged at me for ages. When I glanced over at Joe, the dopey grin on his face told me that he was already in the game. "We'd love to help," he replied. "Do you have any idea who might want to do something like this—and why? I mean, other than a ghost. Their motives are always pretty cut-and-dried—you know, haunting, scaring. That kind of thing."

Adam gave me a searching look, and I shrugged, as if to say, *I accept no responsibility for my brother's ravings.*

"Well," Adam began, "despite being famous, Nathan was a pretty private guy. Heather, too. There weren't a lot of social calls around here—no lavish parties, at least none that I knew of. So his social circle wasn't very big. And with his decline in popularity, he wasn't getting as much press as he used to. That being said, Nathan still enjoyed a certain level of notoriety among horror lovers—particularly other horror writers. Back in his heyday, he always said exactly what was on his mind in interviews. Honest—to a fault. That made him heroic to some people, but not so much to others. So Nathan definitely had enemies—although I can't imagine their reasons for stealing his things and scaring his wife now that he's dead."

I rubbed my chin. Adam was right. What would be the point of doing this now? There had to be a reason. "Let us worry about the motive," I replied. "So, we've got the disgruntled writer option—who else was a part of Nathan's life at the end?"

"Well, there was his longtime publisher; he lives in New York. Steven Lane. Then there's his editor, Michael Hammer, and his literary agent, Peter Huang. Peter's local. They put up with Nathan's radical honesty for decades, but then again, Nathan put them on the map." Adam paused, and then let out a sigh. "And of course there's the band of Foxwood superfans who roam the Internet, still arguing about plot inconsistencies from books Nathan wrote fifteen years ago. God knows what strange urges lurk in the minds of those people. I wouldn't put a stunt like this past one of them."

I nodded. The number of suspects was quickly adding up. "We need to meet some of these people," I said, "and begin ruling things out. When can we start?"

"Tonight," Adam answered. "At midnight. Mrs. Foxwood is holding a memorial for Nathan outside on the grounds. She's going to read an excerpt from the book he finished right before he died, and then spread the ashes. Most of their friends and colleagues will be there, and I'm sure it's been leaked online, so some of the superfans are bound to show up too. It's the perfect opportunity for you guys to sniff around and talk to people."

Joe looked startled. "Wait a minute. The book is finished?" he said. "We heard rumors that Mr. Foxwood was working on a novel about Cliffside Manor, but not that it was completed."

"Yes, well, it's something only a few people know at the moment," Adam explained. "Mrs. Foxwood hasn't spoken to the media since the accident."

Joe gave a sharp nod. "We'll be at the memorial," he said.

"Oh, I almost forgot." Adam pulled out a photograph from his pocket and handed it to us. It showed a young Mr. and Mrs. Foxwood smiling at the camera. It was a close-up with Nathan's arms wrapped around her shoulders. "The watch he's wearing, it's one of the things that went missing. Not only is it valuable but I know Mrs. Foxwood would love to have it back. Nathan really loved it."

Joe and I looked closer. The watch had a regular black wristband but it was the face that was interesting. The hands looked like silver bones and a silver outline of a skull was in the center.

As we walked out of the house and back into the windy, gray day, I couldn't help but wonder who—or what—else would be joining us that night.

MIDNIGHT MAYHEM

3

JOE

DO YOU KNOW WHAT'S SCARIER THAN a haunted house?

A haunted house at midnight!

The woods that huddled around Cliffside Manor were pitch black and full of the sounds of crickets and night birds. Frank and I walked toward the cluster of torches set up along the cliff that gave the house its name, where I could see the faces of a few dozen people lit up by the flickering light, waiting for Nathan Foxwood's memorial service to begin.

The chilly afternoon had turned into a frigid evening, but I was too excited to be cold. This case had my heart racing and my blood pumping like a roller-coaster ride, and things had barely gotten started. Who had stolen those items? Who was frightening people in the manor, and why? As appealing as a vengeful ghost was to me, my instinct was still to agree with Frank. There had to be some kind of ordinary explanation for what was happening.

Still, looking up at that house, the way it loomed in the shadows like a beast waiting to devour anyone who came near . . . It almost made me want to believe in something more supernatural than that.

"Hey," Frank said, interrupting my thoughts. "Isn't that the same reporter from the estate sale?"

I squinted into the darkness and was able to make out the familiar face of Aisha Best, craning her neck to scan the faces in the crowd. "Miss Best," I said, strolling up next to her while Frank grumbled into his collar. "Fancy seeing you twice in one day."

Aisha took one look at me and smiled the smile of a cat who's caught a mouse. "Fancy indeed, Mr. Hardy," she replied. When she saw the surprise on my face at being identified, she continued, "Don't worry, Joe. I'll only blow your cover here if you refuse to tell me what you know. I need my story, after all."

I stumbled back a few paces, my hand to my heart as if I'd been wounded. "And here I thought you looked me up because of my boyish charm," I said.

Aisha chuckled. "I thought you looked familiar when I first laid eyes on you, but I couldn't place you. When I got back to my office, it was a cinch to figure out you and

tall-dark-and-silent over there were none other than the infamous Hardy brothers."

I glanced over at Frank and raised my eyebrows. "Infamous, even!"

"Anyway, I want to know what you know," Aisha said. "This story is blowing up by the hour!"

A moment later a murmur filtered through the crowd as Adam Parker arrived with Heather Foxwood at his side. Aisha took off the instant she saw Mrs. Foxwood, followed by two other reporters, all of them asking the widow for an interview. "People! People!" Adam said, placing himself between the reporters and Mrs. Foxwood. "This is not the time or the place for questions. This is a solemn event— please have some respect!" I noticed that this time, Adam was wearing a black bow tie with little skulls on it. *Does this guy have a bow tie for every occasion?* I wondered.

After Adam's warning, the reporters backed off quietly and let them through the crowd and up to a podium that had been set up right on the cliff side. Mrs. Foxwood, dressed in black, her face like a melancholy moon in the darkness, set a sheaf of papers down on the podium and gazed out to the crowd. "People used to say that my husband was fearless," she began in a strong, resonant voice. "That only a man with an heart of stone could write the things that he did. But no one knew Nathan the way I did. No one could see that he *was* afraid—just as afraid as you and me. Maybe even more so. The difference was that

he didn't run from his monsters. I loved him for that."

Mrs. Foxwood sniffed and shuffled some pages in front of her. "I'd like to read an excerpt from the novel Nathan finished just before his death: *The Haunting of Cliffside Manor*."

An excited whispering went through the audience. Frank leaned over to me and said, "I thought you said that Nathan Foxwood's books haven't been popular in years."

I nodded. "They haven't!"

"Well," Frank said, "I have a feeling that's about to change."

Mrs. Foxwood cleared her throat and started to read. "'With the unholy creature in pursuit,'" she began, "'I dashed through the house, the candlelight piercing the darkness in the hall but not in my heart—where the blackest dread had taken up residence. No one else could see him there, no one understood. But I could see him. And I knew that he would not stop hunting me until I had taken my last breath on this earth.'" As she recited the words, I could swear that the air got a little colder, the wind biting a little more deeply into my collar. All the people around me seemed to notice it too and huddled closer together, hanging on her every word. "'I turned a corner,'" she was saying, "'thinking I had managed to escape the beast—but after throwing the bolt on the door, I spun around to see my death, staring at me with eyes full of fire.'" She stopped then and looked back out to the crowd. A small smile crept onto her face. "Sorry about the cliff-hanger," she said, and the crowd murmured

with excitement. "My husband did always have a flair for the dramatic. Peter? I think it's time." A dapper-looking older man in a three-piece suit came up and handed Mrs. Foxwood a simple silver urn. *That must be Peter Huang, Mr. Foxwood's agent,* I thought. Mrs. Foxwood brought the urn up to her face and seemed to whisper something to it. Then she opened the lid, turned toward the cliff side, and in one graceful sweep, threw the ashes within into the wind.

"Oh my God—*look!*" someone suddenly shouted.

The crowd whirled as one toward the manor. It had been dark during the memorial, but now the central bay window was flooded with light. A shadowy figure was framed there, filling the window with its bulk. A few people in the crowd shrieked in terror. "Adam," I heard Mrs. Foxwood say, her voice hollow. "Who is that?"

Adam was shaking his head in disbelief. "I don't know! The house was empty when I locked up. . . . I don't know!" He and Peter made a move toward the manor, but before they had even taken a few steps, the light went out, and the house was dark once more. "Come on, Peter," Adam said. "They won't get away that easily." Adam jogged up to us. "Joe, Frank—keep an eye on things out here for me while Peter and I search the house. Okay?"

Frank and I nodded, and Adam and Peter ran off.

"What was that, do you think?" I asked Frank.

Frank shook his head. "Another prank, I suspect. But why? What's the point of all these stunts, anyway?"

On the other side of the crowd, Aisha Best caught my eye and waved me over. "She probably wants the scoop right about now," I said. I was about to make my way over there when Frank put a hand on my chest to stop me.

"Let me talk to her, okay, Romeo?" he said. "I can give her the facts just as well as you can."

"What?" I asked. "You think I'll put my foot in my mouth?"

"I'm surprised it isn't already in there," he replied, and left to greet Aisha before I could hit him with a witty comeback.

Ugh, my brother could be *such* a party pooper. I walked over to a table of refreshments to grab a bottled water. Two people stood nearby, hovering over a tray of cubed cheese and crackers. One was a tall, bony man in a black shirt and jeans, his back bowed over the table like a crescent moon as he savagely speared one piece of cheddar after another. Next to him, a rotund woman with a bird's nest of ash-brown hair stood, gripping a cup of punch and watching the crowd with darting eyes. She wore heavy makeup and a somewhat garish brown-and-yellow-striped coat with a fur-lined collar. The two of them reminded me of a crow and a partridge perched side by side on a power line, watching the world pass by below. There was something else about them that seemed familiar, but I couldn't put my finger on what. I sidled up next to them, loading up a plate with fruit and crudités so I could eavesdrop on their conversation.

"A strange party for a strange man—God rest his soul—wouldn't you say, Edwin?" the woman said.

"God's got nothing to do with that man's soul, as far as I'm concerned," the man grumbled, adjusting his circular silver glasses.

The woman put a hand on her chest and opened her mouth in shock. "Edwin! What a thing to say! And at Nathan's memorial, no less!" I noticed that despite her disapproving tone, the corner of her lipsticked mouth turned up in a smirk. "Nathan may have had a big mouth and been one of the most arrogant men I've ever met—*but* he had talent!"

The man called Edwin stabbed an unsuspecting chunk of Monterey Jack before answering. "Pah! Talent. More like a good publicist. His debut was good. Fresh. Everything after that was just the same old thing being served up on a different plate."

Just then a nervous young woman stepped up to the table, a couple of ratty old paperbacks gripped in her hand. "Mr. Queen, Miss Oakentree? I'm so sorry to bother you like this, but do you think I could have your autographs?"

Queen? Oakentree? Now I understood why these two people seemed oddly familiar. I'd seen their faces on the backs of my dad's books! Back in the day, Minerva Oakentree wrote what people called "cozy thrillers," which were like regular thrillers, except with more cats. Edwin Queen was one of Nathan Foxwood's predecessors, an old-school horror writer whose books always got critical acclaim, but never really sold very well. Dad kept some of his books in the house for appearances, but those pages were not nearly as well-worn as the Foxwood novels I used to read.

"Why, I'd be delighted!" the woman—Miss Oakentree—replied, grabbing the pen and one of the books from the young woman's hand. Edwin Queen then signed the other one with barely a glance at the fan.

After the young woman dashed off, a huge smile plastered on her face, the two writers turned back to each other. "Well," said Mr. Queen, "at least there are still some people out there with good taste. All is not lost."

"Oh!" Miss Oakentree piped up. "That reminds me. Did you ever get that watch back from Nathan? The one you two had been fighting over all those years?"

Mr. Queen looked uncomfortable at the question. "No," he finally said. "But the watch isn't all that man took from me. Anyway, I'll get it back in time. I'll get it all back." Suddenly, as if he felt my eyes on him, Mr. Queen swiveled around and speared me with a glance so sharp that I felt like a cube of cheese.

"Um," I said, pulling a small pad of paper and a pen out of my pocket. "Autograph?"

A smile curled up his narrow face and he took my pen. Mr. Queen certainly had a motive. But he was here when the prank in the house happened . . . so could it be that there was more than one disgruntled writer looking to spit on Nathan Foxwood's grave?

I had just thanked Mr. Queen and taken back my paper

and pen when, out of the corner of my eye, I saw a flash of light from the woods. I turned to look, and I could just make out a dim yellow orb of light, moving swiftly through the trees.

Aha!

If someone *had* been playing a prank inside the house, maybe they were trying to make their getaway! Lucky for Adam that Joe Hardy and his eagle eyes stayed behind to keep watch, am I right?

Normally, I would have told Frank where I was going, but he was too far away for me to call out, and I was certain that I'd lose my quarry if I wasted a single second. "Guess I'm flying solo on this one," I muttered to myself, and took off at full speed into the dark, dark woods.

I tried to run silently, quieting my breath and stepping lightly across the mossy ground, hoping that the guy wouldn't hear my approach. It was all going really well— until I stepped right onto a dry branch.

Crack!

The branch snapped with a sound like a thunderclap, and I froze. For an instant, the orb of light went still—and then it went out. And the silence was replaced by the sound of rapid footfalls tearing across the ground and away from me. "Oh no, you don't!" I growled under my breath, and took off after them. I was running full tilt when the woods, well, ended. Abruptly.

"Whoa!" I gasped, stumbling to a halt and windmilling

my arms to regain my balance. Mere feet in front of me was the cliff's edge. Beyond it lay the valley, deep and darker than the night. *That was a close one,* I thought. *But where did he go?* The sound of running feet had stopped completely. I peeked over the edge, trying to make out if there was a ledge or some kind of path leading down the cliff side where my prey might be hiding.

And then there were two hands grabbing my shoulders from behind. My martial arts training kicked in immediately and I swiveled to trap the attacker's wrist and execute a take-down. But whoever it was had momentum—and I never got the chance to show off my judo skills. Within seconds my sneakers had lost purchase on the weedy ground, and I was slipping over the edge—down, down into the abyss.

ON THE SCENT

4

FRANK

CONTRARY TO POPULAR BELIEF, JOE wasn't the only Hardy who could talk to women. At least, that's what I was telling myself as I made my way over to Aisha Best.

She smiled as I approached and extended a hand for me to shake. "Don't trust your brother to talk to the press, hmm? I have heard that he's a bit of a wild card." She chuckled. "You're Frank, right?"

I quickly wiped the sweat off my palm and took her hand. "I'm Frank," I blurted, waggling her arm up and down. *Relax, Hardy!* I scolded myself. *You sound like a robot!* I cleared my throat and soldiered on. "So, what do you want to know?"

"Can you tell me—Oh! Mrs. Foxwood! Mrs. Foxwood! A moment of your time, please!" Halfway through her question to me, Aisha caught sight of Heather Foxwood coming our way, trying to escape the attentions of yet another reporter. One look at Aisha's notebook and cameraman and she had the expression of a cornered animal. Then she saw me.

"Oh, Frank, there you are! I've been looking for you." She turned to Aisha and said, "I'm so sorry, miss, but your interview will have to wait. I have a matter to discuss with Mr. Hardy here." Then she steered me away from the crowd. I craned my head back to look at Aisha and shrugged helplessly. The reporter mouthed back, "Later," and I gave her a thumbs-up.

Mrs. Foxwood stopped at the edge of the crowd and breathed a sigh of relief. "Sorry about that, Frank. But I needed to get some air—the vultures are circling." She looked around at the assembled people—a mixture of fellow horror writers, fans, and assorted business associates, from the looks of them. "Normally I'd get Adam to bail me out of these situations, but he and Peter are still in the manor." She looked up at the place and shivered. "I know it's irrational, but sometimes I wonder if that house did kill my husband. You stay in there long enough, you start to feel like it has a life of its own."

I nodded, unsure of how to respond. "So, I read that you're a research scientist," I ventured, trying to lighten the mood. "I love the study of science—what exactly do you do?"

Mrs. Foxwood brightened. "That's right. I work in a lab in downtown Bayport. Human anatomy."

My eyebrows went up. "You mean dissecting cadavers and things?"

"That's part of it, yes," Mrs. Foxwood said.

"Oh," I replied, feeling a little queasy.

She gave a small grin. "Nathan and I were very different people, but we both had strong stomachs for things that other people might find . . . distasteful."

"Distasteful?" I said, shaking my head. "Oh, no. No, no, no . . . no . . ."

Mrs. Foxwood laughed. "I think you doth protest too much."

I shrugged, smiling. "I *might* be a little squeamish. Just a little. Anyway, it sounds like a great job."

Mrs. Foxwood crossed her arms and sighed. "Well, I needed a great job. You'd be amazed how much it costs to keep up an old place like this." She shook her head. "When we moved in, the plumbing leaked, the electricity was spotty at best, there was mold in the basement—" At that moment, a familiar sound reached my ear from the depths of the forest. It was a long whistle, starting high, then going low, then ending on another high note. It was the SOS signal that my brother and I used from time to time, in case we ever got separated.

Joe was in trouble.

"I'm sorry, Mrs. Foxwood," I stammered. "Gotta run!" And I took off into the woods toward the sound.

Branches snagged my clothes as I ran through the darkness,

my feet slipping and sliding on the carpet of damp, fallen leaves. Joe's whistle got louder as I went—I must be going the right way. "Joe!" I shouted. "I'm coming! Where are you?"

"This way, Frank!" Joe's voice was close. I turned toward it and saw a clearing ahead. I was about to burst out of the trees at full speed when Joe's voice rang out again, this time from immediately in front of me. "Frank, stop! Stop!"

I skidded to a halt just in time to realize that I'd reached the edge of the cliff, and Joe was hanging off it, his hands gripping a cluster of weeds. The weeds were snapping one by one—within seconds, the weeds would give way and Joe would be gone.

"Hold on!" I shouted, and dove to the ground with my arms outstretched, like a baseball runner diving for home base. Just as the last bunch of weeds gave way, I grabbed Joe by the wrists and held on tight. My arm and shoulder muscles screamed with the sudden weight of Joe's entire body, but I didn't let go. Joe swung in midair, scrabbling for purchase on the cliff side with his feet. At last he managed to find a foothold in the rocks, and with that added momentum, I was able to loop my hands under his arms and haul him back to solid ground. We both lay there in the dirt for a minute, just panting and staring up at the moon.

"What took you so long?" Joe finally asked.

I sat up and looked at him in disbelief. "Are you kidding me? I just saved your butt!"

"It's a good thing I told you to slow down, or else you

36

would have sailed over the edge too and we'd *both* be out of luck."

I crossed my arms and glared, hoping he could see my expression in the moonlight. Joe looked at me and laughed. "I just can't help myself sometimes." He slapped me on the back. "Thanks, bro. My butt owes you one."

I snorted. "So, what happened, anyway? Why are you in the woods hanging off the side of a cliff?"

Joe filled me in on the light he'd seen in the woods, and how someone had shoved him over the edge. "Whoever it was," he finished, "I bet it's the same person playing these pranks and stealing stuff from the manor."

I was about to reply when there was a rustling in the woods behind us. I whirled around to see the outline of a dark shape turn and retreat through the trees. "Did you see that?" I asked Joe. "Whoever it was might still be here!"

Without another word, Joe and I leaped to our feet and took off after the figure—but by the time we reached the area where we'd spotted him, there was no trace of him anywhere. The woods had gone silent once again. I swung the beam of my phone's flashlight all around us, but it revealed nothing but trees. "This is definitely where he was standing," I said, noting the broken branches and footprints in the dirt. "But we lost him."

"Darn!" Joe said, kicking at the ground. "So close! I wonder why he stuck around after pushing me off the cliff. Seems like a weird thing to do, don't you think?"

"Hey, what's that?" I said as my flashlight's beam caught something bright red on the ground in front of us. I bent to pick it up—it was a pin in the shape of a skull, with the words *FOXWOOD FAN CLUB* written on it in black lettering. "He must have dropped it when he took off."

Joe plucked it from my fingers and smiled. "It looks like a clue to me."

I grinned back. "Right. Let's get back to the others. Maybe Adam can tell us more."

We trekked back through the woods to where the memorial had been held. On the way, Joe told me about the conversation he'd overheard between the two horror writers, Minerva Oakentree and Edwin Queen, and how Mr. Queen had referenced a watch that he'd never gotten back from Mr. Foxwood, as well as something else that Mr. Foxwood had supposedly taken from him.

"What do you think he could have meant?" I asked. "Fame? Money?"

"Could be either of those," Joe replied. "Or maybe a *lady*." He waggled his eyebrows meaningfully.

"But Mr. and Mrs. Foxwood have been married for a million years, haven't they?" I asked.

"Roughly a million," Joe agreed. "But maybe it happened a long time ago, before that. Edwin Queen looks like the kind of guy who could hold a grudge."

"Fair enough," I said. "But we know he couldn't have done the prank in the house, because he was at the memorial

with us. So even if he's a suspect, he'd have to be working with someone else."

Joe nodded. We finally cleared the tree line and were back in civilization. Almost everyone had left the memorial by now, but Adam Parker was still there, stacking folding chairs and picking up some stray trash left behind by the guests. He ran over as soon as he caught sight of us.

"Where have you guys been?" Adam asked. "Peter and I found exactly nothing at the manor, and when we got back here, there was no sign of you two. Mrs. Foxwood said she saw you running off into the woods, Frank."

Joe and I caught Adam up on what had happened, and his eyes got wide when we told him about Joe's close call on the cliff side. "So I was right!" Adam said. "Someone *is* behind all this trouble. Someone much more real than the Gray Hunter."

"Well," Joe broke in, "we can't *totally* rule out supernatural interference. I mean, the figure in the woods *did* seem to disappear into thin air."

"You can't be serious," I told him.

"I'm a *little* serious . . . ," Joe replied.

I rolled my eyes. "Anyway, we found this pin on the ground, and we think it might help lead us to the culprit. Do you know anything about the Foxwood Fan Club?"

Adam took the pin from my hand and inspected it closely. "It's a small group," he said, "but it's been going on for many years, so there are plenty of people this could have belonged to. If you want to know more about it, you'd have to ask either Peter Huang or Mrs. Foxwood. One of them should have access to the fan club records."

I nodded. "Okay then, we'll split up. Tomorrow morning, I'll go see Heather Foxwood at her lab, and Joe, you can visit Peter Huang at his office. Don't worry, Adam, we'll get to the bottom of this."

"I hope you do," Adam replied. "Because let me tell you—this whole heart-attack-a-day thing isn't doing me much good. I'd rather be reading a ghost story than living one."

It was close to two a.m. by the time Joe and I got back to the car. I should have been exhausted, but my mind was spinning with questions, making me feel wide awake. Who was doing the haunting at Cliffside Manor—and why?

SPYING EYES 5

JOE

WHEN I IMAGINED THE KIND OF place that a hotshot agent would work at, it looked nothing like this. I expected a sleek, modern kind of building—all steel and glass and fancy elevators and marble floors. But driving up to Mr. Foxwood's agent's office the next morning, what I actually found was a squat brown building with tiny, circular windows that looked like some sort of aging undersea vessel. I parked in the weed-infested lot and made my way to the entrance, scanning the yellowed directory for the name Peter Huang.

"Third floor," I muttered to myself. I headed to the elevator but changed my mind when I got a look at it. The up button was cracked through, and the lights at the top of the elevator kept blinking on and off in an unsettling way. I mean, danger is fun and all, but I don't have a death wish. I took the stairs.

Up on the third floor, I walked to the end of the hall until I found a door with a sign reading PETER HUANG LITERARY AGENCY. I knocked on the door—and something unexpected happened. The door just swung right open.

"Um . . . hello?" I called out. No answer. I took a step inside the office and poked my head around the door. It wasn't very large at all, just a single room with a tiny bathroom off to the side and a coat closet. The place looked like a hurricane had blown through it—folders and papers and books piled helter-skelter on every surface, sticky notes covered in chicken scratch pasted along the walls, chipped mugs perched here and there on shelves and desktops, filled with coffee of indeterminate age. There was a lot to look at—but no Peter Huang.

I sighed. *Probably should have called first,* I thought. But hey, hindsight is 20/20. Figuring that the agent was probably just out to lunch, I decided to wait around a while until he came back. I went to close the door again—but not before I spied something sitting on the top of a heaping pile on Huang's desk.

A folder labeled *FOXWOOD NEW NOVEL.*

My heart leaped. The little devil on my shoulder immediately began whispering in my ear. *Nathan Foxwood's new novel! The book only one or two other people in the world have read, and it's right there. . . . Who would know if I took a little peek?*

Usually the little angel on the other shoulder pipes up around this time, to tell me why whatever thing I was aiming to do was a superbad idea and could get me into such and such trouble—but today the little angel was just like, *Yeah, man, go for it!*

Okay, so my little angel may not be as angelic as other people's, but still—what was the worst that could happen? I quickly scanned the hallway for anyone coming, but the place was as silent as a tomb. With the coast clear, I snuck into the office and quietly closed the door behind me. I'd just check out the pages for a few minutes, just for the thrill of it, and then I'd scoot right back outside and wait for Huang to show up. Easy peasy.

I opened the folder and looked at the first page. *The Haunting of Cliffside Manor*, it read. *A Novel by Nathan Foxwood*. Some of the letters were uneven, with little ink smears here and there along the paper—evidence of being written on an old-fashioned typewriter, something Mr. Foxwood was notorious for. It was kind of a crazy thing to do, given how much better a laptop and a decent printer would work—but at the same time, there was something amazing about seeing the book written out this way. It made that pile of paper so much more valuable, knowing that it was the only one, and knowing that every letter was formed by the force of Mr. Foxwood's own fingers across the keys.

As I started to read, I felt myself fall under the spell of the story, as I always did when I read his books. I must have lost track of time, because the next thing I knew, I was hearing footsteps and voices coming down the hall—coming right for the very office I was standing in.

I glanced up at the clock on the wall. Yikes, I'd been in there for almost half an hour! I thought about trying to slip back out into the hallway, but it was too late—the outline of a figure had already appeared outside the frosted glass of the office door.

Could I have stood my ground and merely played dumb upon being caught inside the man's office? Used my charming personality to weasel my way out of getting into trouble? Made up some story about *really* needing to use the bathroom? Sure, I could have. But what did I do instead?

I hid inside the closet.

Look, I'm not proud. But what can I say? My survival instincts took over, and the closet was there.

I dived in among half a dozen trench coats and suit jackets, narrowly avoiding being impaled on the point of an umbrella before I managed to shut the door behind me. Mere seconds later, I heard the office door swing open with a squeak, followed by the sound of footsteps on the wooden floor. "Look, Steve," said a smooth male voice. "I know the sales of Foxwood's books have tanked over the past five years—but you have to believe me, this book, it's going to be different!"

That must be Peter, I thought. *Steve . . . the name sounds familiar. Oh! Steven Lane—Nathan Foxwood's publisher!*

Adam told us about him. I pressed my eye up against a crack in the door and peered out into the office. I could see what must have been Peter's hands gesticulating from where he was standing in front of another person, an older man with thinning white hair and artsy-looking eyeglasses. "Have you no tact?" Steve said. "The man is still warm in his grave and you're already talking about cash flow. I flew in from New York for the memorial, not to listen to your sales pitch. Besides, just because Nathan Foxwood is dead, that doesn't mean that his books will suddenly become hot again. We might get a little spike for a month or two, but after that, people will just forget about him again. Face it, Peter—his time is over. Move on. Anyway, Edwin Queen called me the other day. I know he's old news himself, but he says that he's got a new project ready—something sellable for a change. With Nathan gone, we've got a gap in the horror list. I'm thinking of giving him a chance."

"Edwin Queen?!" Peter sputtered. "The only horror writer whose murder scenes could put you to sleep? Steve, please, listen to me. If you'd said this to me two months ago, I'd have agreed with you. But things have changed. The man died in a fiery car crash right outside an infamous haunted house. This isn't just a novel anymore"—I watched the agent place one hand on the manuscript—"it's a whole melodrama that is unfolding *as we speak.*" He proceeded to regale the publisher with the story of all the "hauntings" going on at the manor in the past few days, and the media frenzy that's been growing around them. He spoke with a level of zeal that immediately made me suspicious. There had been some thefts and an attempted assault on Mrs. Foxwood—and yet Peter talked as if it was the best thing that could have happened.

"And you say that the novel is actually about the history of the manor? The murders and this supposed madman?" Steve asked. The tone of his voice had changed—now he sounded interested.

"Exactly," Huang said. "Talk about life imitating art. It's perfect; people are already frothing at the mouth to read it! We practically had to beat them off with a stick at the memorial. I mean, don't get me wrong"—here, Peter's voice became low and subdued—"Nathan's death was a terrible loss. But you have to admit, with all this going on, the guy is worth more dead than alive."

I watched as Steve shook his head and chuckled humorlessly. "Peter, I always said you had a dollar sign where your heart should be. But I'll bite. How about a hundred-thousand-copy first printing for Foxwood's book?"

"Fantastic!" Huang said, clapping his hands. "I think this calls for a drink." I watched as the agent walked over to a crowded shelf and unearthed two glasses and a bottle of amber-colored something. He poured a little of it into each glass and handed one to Steve.

"To Nathan Foxwood!" Huang announced, raising his glass.

As the two men clinked their drinks, something terrible happened.

I sneezed.

Now, I was fast enough to bury my face in one of the guy's suit jackets as I did it (sorry, Peter), so it wasn't loud—but it was loud enough.

"What was that?" Steve asked. "Sounds like it came from the closet." I held my breath.

"Ah, probably a mouse," Peter said. "I've been dealing with a lot of vermin in here lately."

Whew, I thought. *That was close.*

"Well, that's no surprise," Steve sneered. "Look at this place. It's a sty. Dust bunnies everywhere . . ."

I heard Peter sigh. "Yes, well, it's all I've been able to afford these past couple years. But hey—if I'm right about this book, maybe I'll be back in my uptown office again. Just like the good old days!"

All that talk of dust bunnies made my nose start to tickle again, so I was quite relieved when I heard the rustling of coats and feet moving toward the door. "Let me take you out to lunch before you go back to the city, Steve," Huang was saying. "It's on me!"

A moment later I heard the door close behind them. I counted out a full sixty seconds before slowly emerging from the closet. I brushed the dust and grime from my clothes, sighed, and then sneezed violently three times in a row. Well, I was no closer to finding out who the Foxwood Fan

Club pin belonged to, but eavesdropping on Peter made me think he might make a pretty good suspect himself. Not only was he benefiting from Mr. Foxwood's untimely death, but now this haunting business had Nathan Foxwood's name plastered all over the papers and the Internet! The best possible publicity for the upcoming book. Peter barely had to lift a finger to sell the new book—it was certain to be a bestseller, just as he'd said.

Could it be that all of this wasn't just good luck coming Peter's way? Could it be that after Mr. Foxwood died, Peter took it upon himself to create this hype in order to take advantage of the moment and get his own career back on the road to success? It sure seemed like a possibility.

I thought back to the events that had occurred, and other than the cliff incident at the memorial, Peter could have potentially committed them all. Maybe he had an accomplice who somehow got into the house last night and put on the show during Mrs. Foxwood's speech? Then Peter could have let them escape when he went with Adam to investigate. It would be a good way to throw suspicion away from Peter! It all started to make sense.

I hurried back to the car, eager to get back to Frank and share this new information. I still hadn't found out where the Foxwood Fan Club came from, but I believed I'd found something much better.

THE BONE FACTORY

6

FRANK

SECOND DOOR ON THE LEFT," I MUTTERED to myself as I walked down the cold, stark white hallway of BBL, otherwise known as the Bayport Bio Laboratory. As passionate as I am about the scientific method, I'd never had a good reason to step foot into the place until today—but now that I was here, I was pretty pumped to scope the place out. I had been told by the receptionist that Heather Foxwood was still in a meeting, and that I should just wait in the lobby, but I'd had about a gallon of coffee that morning and needed to use the bathroom.

"It's through the double doors and down that hallway," the young woman had said. "Second door on the left."

A rush of cool air hit me as I'd passed through the

double doors, leaving the warm, carpeted lobby to enter the sterile environment of the lab. I couldn't help peeking into the tiny windows of the doors I passed on the way, catching sight of scientists in white coats and safety goggles working with huge steel machines that hummed and churned so powerfully that I could feel it through the soles of my shoes. *So cool*, I thought. *Maybe one day I'll give up all this crime fighting for a job solving the mysteries of the universe instead.*

My mind wandering through fantasies of winning a Nobel Prize, I came to a door on the left and opened it. To my surprise, the bathroom was pitch black inside—but then again, maybe it was equipped with one of those energy-saving, motion-detecting light switches. Leaving the door open for light, I took a step inside and waved my arms around in the darkness, but nothing happened. (Except me looking like an idiot to the two pretty young scientists who passed by as I did this.) I tried to find the switch on the wall, but that didn't work either. Finally I took out my phone and switched on the flashlight function.

"Ahh!!!"

I leaped backward and yelped in a less-than-awesome way as my flashlight illuminated the wide-open mouth and hollow eyes of a human skull less than three feet from my face. The beam of my flashlight bounced around with the movement, revealing other skulls and bones lined up on shelves and labeled with tiny, neat handwriting.

"Found our storage closet, have you, Mr. Hardy?" said a voice behind me.

I ordered my heart to slow down as I turned to see Heather Foxwood watching me from right outside the door, wearing a white lab coat over a steel-gray dress, a small, amused smile touching her lips.

I stepped out of the closet, feeling a warm blush climb up my neck. "The receptionist said the men's room was the second door on the left . . . ," I managed.

"I'm sure she did. This is the third one."

I looked back down the hall. I had been so preoccupied with my daydreams of being an award-winning scientist that I'd counted wrong. "Well," I said, trying to salvage a bit of my dignity, "I have to say, that was only the second scariest bathroom I've been in. Which is saying something."

After making a quick stop at the actual men's room, I met Mrs. Foxwood back in the hallway, where she led me farther into the depths of the laboratory. "So, what can I do for you, Frank? The message you left said it had something to do with what's going on in the manor? I told Adam that I didn't want any more fuss over this. The media is already hammering at my door every moment of the day—"

"I promise you, Mrs. Foxwood," I broke in, "my brother and I are looking into this with the utmost discretion. Last night, during the memorial, we were on the trail of someone in the woods who we think may be responsible for the thefts and disturbances at Cliffside. It was too dark to identify them, but we did find this." I pulled out the pin and handed it to her.

"A fan club pin," she mused, turning it over in her hands. "So you think some kind of obsessed superfan is behind all of this?"

"It's possible," I agreed. "It fits the MO of the crimes. Obviously the things taken from the house would have monetary value, but they would mean a lot more to someone familiar with Mr. Foxwood and his work."

Mrs. Foxwood nodded solemnly. "I can show you how to access the fan club database on my office computer. Perhaps you'll find what you're searching for there. I warn you, though, there are thousands of names. Finding the owner of that pin will be like looking for a needle in a haystack."

I smiled. "I like a challenge."

At that point, we'd reached the end of the long hallway and pushed through another set of double doors. Beyond them was a large open space, filled with even larger machines—some the size of a minivan—and dozens of steel vats. "So," Mrs. Foxwood said, changing the subject. "What do you make of the Bio Lab?"

"It's amazing," I replied, casting my gaze around the room. "What exactly do you do here?"

"My department specializes in diseases of the skeletal system," she answered. "We conduct experiments on diseased cells, looking for cures and testing out new medicines before they go to market. My job is to isolate certain cells and replicate them for testing."

"Skeletal system, eh," I said. "Hence the bones."

"Hence the bones, yes," she echoed. "We have a nickname for the lab around here: the Bone Factory."

I nodded with interest, scrutinizing the labels on the steel vats as we passed by. Methanol, sulfuric acid, sodium hydride, something called ZnS. ZnS . . . the Z would be for zinc, but I couldn't think of what the rest of the compound would be. I was pretty good with chemistry, though, so I was certain it would come back to me at some point. "I'm guessing these vats contain the chemicals you all use for your experiments?" I asked.

"Right," Mrs. Foxwood said. "You'd be surprised how much sulfuric acid it takes to dissolve an entire human body."

My eyes must have grown to the size of dinner plates, because Mrs. Foxwood looked at me and laughed. "Oh, Mr. Hardy—I'm just having a little fun at your expense. You don't stay married to a horror writer for all those years and not develop a bit of a dark sense of humor."

"Right, of course," I said, chuckling.

We finally arrived at Mrs. Foxwood's office, which was immaculately neat and decorated with photographs of her and her husband in happier times—vacationing in Hawaii, standing arm in arm in front of a stone church on their wedding day. There was also a framed dedication page from one of Mr. Foxwood's novels. It read: *To Heather:*

Even death cannot part us. She caught me looking at it and a strange expression crossed her face—a bittersweet kind of smile. Then the moment was over, and she leaned over the computer on her desk, clicking around until she'd brought up the fan club database on the screen. "It's all yours," she said, straightening and gesturing for me to sit down.

I cracked my knuckles and got to work. As Mrs. Foxwood had said, the database contained about four thousand names spanning the decade that Mr. Foxwood's books had been popular. Using the expanded search function, I first narrowed down the list to members living in Bayport. I figured it was a safe bet that the perpetrator was local—otherwise it was unlikely that they'd have the knowledge and access to commit multiple crimes spanning several days. That cut the list down to only a hundred or so! But a hundred suspects was still far too many. I took another look at the pin—a red skull with black lettering. "Has the design of the pin always been the same?" I asked Mrs. Foxwood.

She drummed her fingers on the desk. "Hmm, I think so. At least, mostly the same. It may have changed a little over the years, whenever they had to reorder for new members."

I bit my lip. "Does this database include any photographs?" I asked.

"Actually, yes," Mrs. Foxwood replied. "After they joined, we always asked new members to send in a picture of themselves holding their favorite Nathan Foxwood novel.

Peter used to use them for publicity when Nathan's career was at its peak."

I found the little camera icon next to each member's listing and clicked on one. The first guy had joined the club seven years ago, but he wasn't wearing his pin in the photograph. But the third picture showed a woman who had joined four years ago, and she had the pin on her lapel. Zooming in on the image, I could see that the skull was longer and narrower than the one I had. Another picture showed a man's pin from nine years ago—it was definitely a darker shade of red, and the lettering was in a different typeface. When I checked the rest of the local members, I found a kid who had joined in just the past year, and his pin looked exactly like the one in my hand. He was about my age and had a rebellious smirk on his face. "Max Kingsley," I read. "It looks like he's the only local member to have joined in the past year—no, scratch that. There's one more, another guy named Gavin Cook. Look at their addresses; they live on the same street." I turned to Mrs. Foxwood. "Do you know if new pins were ordered in the past year?"

Mrs. Foxwood nodded. "I think so. I remember Peter asking me whether it was necessary, because there were so few new members joining."

"This is it, then," I said, slapping my hand on the desk with finality. "It's a long shot, but I think Joe and I should pay these two a visit." A moment later I felt my phone vibrate in my pocket. I fished it out and answered. "Joe! Speak of the devil. I've got a lead."

"Oh good," Joe's voice replied. "*Achoo!* What have you got?"

"I went through the list of Foxwood Fan Club members and managed to narrow it down to two likely suspects. Pick me up at the lab and we'll head over to where they live. It's just across town."

"Okay, on my way. *Achoo!*"

"Why are you sneezing?" I asked.

There was a long silence. "It's a long story," Joe finally said.

I hung up with Joe and turned to Mrs. Foxwood. "I think I've got what I need for now," I told her. "Thanks for all your help."

"But of course," Mrs. Foxwood said with a smile. "Here, let me walk you out." She led me back out through the lab to the lobby and out the front door. We said our goodbyes, but before I could turn away, Mrs. Foxwood grabbed my arm. "Mr. Hardy," she said. "Look. I can see you have a scientific mind, like me. I know that you dismiss what you cannot explain. But I have seen things that defy logic and reason—I am convinced that those things killed my husband. Like a scientist, I know you must follow the evidence where it leads you. But whatever you do, please . . . just be careful. I don't want someone else to get hurt."

It was strange and unsettling to hear such things coming out of the mouth of a scientist, and I'd be lying if I said it didn't make me a little nervous about stepping foot inside the manor ever again. But I quickly shook off the feeling, assuring myself that this was a brilliant woman who had just endured quite a trauma, so it was understandable that she would choose to project those fears onto something like a ghostly presence. It gave her someone to blame for her sorrow.

"Don't worry, Mrs. Foxwood," I said. "We'll be careful."

She nodded, and I turned to walk away, deciding to hang out at a café a few doors down to wait for Joe to arrive. I had only made it about a dozen steps before I heard someone's voice call out, "Heather—wait!"

I turned to see a tall, older man dashing across the street toward the lab building. Mrs. Foxwood was halfway through the door when she stopped and caught sight of him. "Edwin?" I heard her reply.

The man stopped in front of the building, and Mrs. Foxwood stepped back out to meet him. Curious, I slipped into a somewhat stinky and rat-infested alleyway next to the lab building to eavesdrop on the conversation.

"What are you doing here?" I heard Mrs. Foxwood say. She sounded somewhat impatient.

"I had to see you," the man replied. "I wanted to talk at the memorial, but there wasn't any time."

"I have to get back to work, Edwin," Mrs. Foxwood said. "Please, whatever it is, make it quick."

Suddenly it came to me that this must be Edwin Queen,

the writer Joe had told me about at the memorial. Joe had said that Mr. Queen had a grudge against Nathan Foxwood.

There was a pause. I almost felt sorry for poor Mr. Queen—I could imagine those piercing blue eyes of hers didn't make it easy for him to think. "Um," he finally managed. "Well, I know it's only been a week since Nathan passed, but I know things haven't been safe in the manor ever since. I don't know where you're staying, but I just wanted you to know that there's a guest room at my place, should you ever need it." He said the entire speech quite rapidly, as if he was both trying to obey her command to be fast, and also get it over with as quickly as possible.

"That's . . . very sweet of you, Edwin, thank you," Mrs. Foxwood said, her tone gracious. "But my accommodations are set for now. If anything changes, I'll be sure to let you know. It was nice to see you again."

After a moment, I heard the click of the lab building door closing. I peeked out of the alleyway to see Mr. Queen standing in front of the door, looking like a dog left out in the cold. He stared into the building after Mrs. Foxwood for a moment, and then took off back across the street, viciously kicking a rock as he went.

My mind awhirl, I entered the café and ordered a hot chocolate. As I sipped, I wondered about Max Kingsley, Gavin Cook, and Edwin Queen. Edwin Queen certainly was an interesting character—could Joe have unwittingly hit upon the truth when he said Queen might have lost a lady to

Nathan Foxwood? It certainly seemed like Queen was going after Mrs. Foxwood with her husband so recently gone. And his mention of things not being safe in the manor lately was suspicious too—could he be doing all this in order to drive Heather Foxwood back into his arms?

It was all possible, but the fact was—at the moment it was Max Kingsley and Gavin Cook that the evidence pointed to. I couldn't ignore the fan club pin, not until we had an explanation for it.

I saw the car pull up outside and quickly went back to the cashier to order another hot chocolate. I knew better than to climb into the car without a hot beverage for each of us. Tracking down suspects works up quite a thirst.

THE TRAP IS SET

7

JOE

"THAT'S IT," FRANK SAID, POINTING TO an ordinary-looking house at the end of the road. "Max Kingsley's house."

I pulled the car slowly up to the curb and parked. "I don't know about this, Frank. I still think Peter is a better bet." I'd filled Frank in on my adventure at Peter Huang's office and my suspicions about his involvement in the crimes.

"Well, well, well," Frank said, turning to me. "We've got no shortage of suspects, it turns out." He then told me what he'd seen with Heather Foxwood and Edwin Queen. "Queen looks pretty good for it too, in my book. I agree that Peter's got a lot of motive also, but you said yourself that he couldn't have been the one up in the house during the memorial. In fact, neither could Queen. He was at the memorial too—you saw him. Furthermore, neither of them could have been the one who shoved you over the cliff side and dropped the fan club pin."

"True," I admitted. "But they could have had an accomplice. Two people could have pulled this off, easy."

"Well then, what if one of those accomplices was either Max Kingsley or Gavin Cook? That doesn't fit as well for Edwin Queen, but if Peter had the list of fan club members, he might have known a few of them himself."

My eyebrows shot up. "Oh!" I said. "I hadn't thought of that."

Frank elbowed me in the ribs. "See? You just have to have a little more faith in your big bro." He folded his arms and looked insufferably proud of himself.

"Humph," I huffed. "Don't get a big head about it. You just came up with the idea right now!"

He shrugged. "Doesn't make it any less awesome. So we'll talk to these superfans, and then go from there."

"Now, are you sure that these are our guys?" I asked.

"I made a few assumptions in my deductions, so I'm not a hundred percent certain," Frank admitted. "But they sure do look good for it. The pin fits, and this house—and Gavin's, down the street—are only a couple of miles from Cliffside Manor. And for what it's worth, Max already has a record, I checked. Minor stuff like petty larceny, vandalism . . . but still. It shows the potential for criminal activity."

I nodded. "It's enough for us to check these guys out, at least. You got a plan, bro?"

Frank bit his lip. "Well—"

"No?" I broke in. "Good, because I do."

Frank rolled his eyes. "Can you not go all James Bond on this situation, please? Can you just not?"

"Frank, *Frank!*" I replied, feigning offense. "Come on, now. Don't you trust me? When have I ever let things get out of hand?" Frank looked down and started counting silently on his fingers. "Don't answer that!" I snapped. "Anyway, it will be fine. You'll see. I'm going to infiltrate the house—you just stay here and keep watch. If something does go awry, I'll give you the signal for backup. Now, just let me have the pin."

Frank dropped the pin into my hand, giving me a *don't screw this up* look.

Pfft, I thought, getting out of the car. *I got this.* I pinned the little skull to my jacket, walked straight up to the door, and knocked. After a minute or so, the door cracked open and a face appeared. The kid was about my age, tall and lanky, sporting a crooked, slept-on black Mohawk and a red T-shirt. "What?" he said, without ceremony.

"Hi, there. You're Max Kingsley, right?" I asked.

"So?" he replied.

Quite the master conversationalist, I thought.

"My name is Owen Hadley, and like you, I'm a member of the Foxwood Fan Club." I gestured to the pin on my jacket.

Max eyed it. "Okay," he said.

"I just joined a few months ago, and some of the other members and I are trying to put together a film project about Nathan Foxwood's life. The president of the fan club mentioned that we should use you as a resource and told me where to find you—she said that you're an expert on this stuff. Sorry to just show up like this, but I was in the neighborhood and was eager to meet you. Would it be cool if we talked for a bit?"

As soon as I'd said the word "expert," I could see the expression on the kid's face change. "Yeah, man, of course," Max said, throwing the door wide open, suddenly full of enthusiasm. "Come right in. I happen to consider myself a preeminent Foxwood scholar, so you've come to the right place."

This guy, I thought, resisting a hard eye roll and walking inside.

Max led me to his room, where another guy with curly brown hair reclined on a ratty couch, rocking out to some grunge metal playing on his laptop. Framed posters of Nathan Foxwood's movies lined the walls, and I could see a bunch of well-read paperbacks peeking out from under an empty pizza box. The one window in the room was pushed open, probably to air out the smell of old food and two guys who probably didn't shower enough. The guy on the couch sat up when I came in, pulling the earbuds from his ears. "Who's this?" he asked Max.

"Owen," Max replied, "from the fan club. He's making a movie and wants our *expert* opinion." He turned back to me. "This is my buddy Gavin. He's a scholar too—knows everything there is to know about the early Foxwood books, the stuff he wrote before he got famous."

Gavin nodded sagely. "It's *very* experimental," he said.

"Uh-huh," I mumbled, meanwhile thinking what a coincidence it was that our two suspects were friends. Then something else grabbed my attention. "Hey, Max," I said brightly. "That is a killer watch you've got."

Max glanced at the wristwatch he was wearing. It was all black except for the silver, bone-shaped hands and the silver outline of a skull on its face. "Oh, this?" he said, a hint of nervousness creeping into his voice. "Yeah, I got it for my birthday."

Liar, I thought. *You got it from Cliffside Manor. That's Nathan Foxwood's watch.* I remembered it from the picture that Adam Parker had shown us. "I bet experts like you guys have some first editions, too, don't you?" I said, trying to lure some of the other stolen items out into the open. "Man, what I'd do to get my hands on an original Foxwood!"

Max hesitated, but Gavin barreled forward, spurred on by my enthusiasm. "Heck yeah, we've got one!" he said, launching himself off the couch and opening up Max's closet. He rummaged through some stuff in a pile before emerging with an old but well-preserved book in his hand. "Check *this* out."

"Wow," I breathed, genuinely impressed. It was an original copy of *The One I Left Alive*, the book that made Nathan Foxwood a household name about twenty years ago. "This has got to be worth thousands of bucks by now."

"It sure is," Gavin agreed. "Pretty cool, right?"

Max, meanwhile, said nothing. He was looking at me with a strange expression on his face. "Haven't I seen you somewhere before, Owen?" he asked.

Uh-oh.

"Me?" I asked, all innocence. "I don't know. I don't think so. Maybe at one of the fan club meetings?"

Max shook his head. "I haven't been to a meeting in ages. And you said you just joined a few months ago."

I nodded. "That's true. Maybe at school? Do you guys go to Bayport High?"

"No . . . ," Max mumbled, still staring at my face, deep in thought.

I had to get out of there and regroup before things went south. These guys were definitely our perps, so now all we had to do was call the cops to collect them. "Well, hey, you guys look like you're pretty busy, so maybe I'll come around again later to ask you about the movie stuff." I turned around to beat a hasty exit when Max's voice stopped me in my tracks.

"Wait," he said.

I swallowed and turned around.

"Now I know who you are," Max went on, all the

friendliness gone from his face. "I've seen your face in the paper. You're one of those brothers, the Hardys. You guys caught that jewelry thief a couple of months ago."

Gavin looked down at the book in his hand. He leaned over to set it down carefully on the couch, before picking up a baseball bat from the floor.

Well, things certainly had taken a turn.

"Listen, guys," I said with a warning in my voice. "It's over. If you turn yourselves in now, it will be better for you. Don't make things worse than they already are."

"The way I see it," Gavin replied, slapping the meaty part of the bat into his palm. "You're outnumbered, Hardy, two to one. If it's gonna be over for anybody, I think that's you."

Without a word, Gavin lunged, bringing the bat swinging down toward me. I sidestepped out of its trajectory, and as it whiffed past my body I reached out and grabbed Gavin's right wrist, twisting it backward and forcing him to drop the weapon. He cried out in pain but recovered quickly, yanking his arm away and barreling into me like a linebacker. The momentum slammed me into the wall of the room, causing a couple of the movie posters to fall from the wall with a crash.

The force took my breath away, but only for an instant. I spun out to prevent him from pinning me to the wall, putting some space between us. His next move was to reach out with his right hand and grab me by the collar.

Big mistake, buddy.

If the martial arts classes I took taught me anything, it's that if an opponent is dumb enough to give you a gift, you should take it.

I grabbed his wrist with both my hands, whirled around to put my back into him, and threw him over with one fluid motion. He hit the floor with a resounding boom. His mouth opened, but no sound came out except a long, low groan.

Max took one look at his friend laid out on the floor and turned tail. He dashed from the room and pounded toward the front door. I was about to take off after him when, from the floor, Gavin reached for my ankle and pulled it out from under me. I went down.

"You just don't give up, do you!" I said through gritted teeth as Gavin tried to put me in a chokehold.

I heard the front door slam. Max had flown the coop! I had to stop him.

"Frank!" I shouted at the top of my lungs. Thank goodness that window was open. Hopefully my voice would carry for some distance. *"Quick, Frank! Don't let him get away!"*

ON THE RUN

8

FRANK

T HAD BEEN A GOOD TEN MINUTES SINCE JOE had walked into Max Kingsley's house, and I'd had my fill of waiting. I was walking across the flagstones up to the front door, working out a plan in my head, when Joe's shout shattered the silence of the suburban street.

"Quick, Frank!" Joe's voice seemed to be coming from the side of the house. *"Don't let him get away!"*

For about five seconds, I wondered who Joe was talking about. Then the answer came rocketing out of the front door and crashing straight into me. Max—for that's who it was, I recognized him from the fan club picture— had enough momentum going that with one shove, I went sprawling into a flower bed. "Hey!" I yelled, leaping back up the moment after I hit the ground. But even still, I wasn't fast enough. Max had already made it to a motorbike that was leaning against the garage and jumped on. By the time I got close, Max had revved the engine and was tearing down the driveway toward me. I dived out of the way at the last possible moment and found myself reclining in yet another flower bed while Max sped down the street toward a dirt path leading into a thicket of trees.

Knock me down once, shame on me.

Knock me down twice . . .

Getting back to my feet, I spied a second motorbike leaning not far from where the first one had been. I ran over, threw myself astride it, and caught another break—the key was in the ignition! With a roar of the engine, I took off in pursuit.

The dirt path into the woods started out smooth but quickly became steep and treacherous with rocks and fallen branches. I gritted my teeth and white-knuckled the handlebars, fighting to keep the bike steady as I sped to catch up with Max. I could hear his engine in the distance and could see flashes of his red T-shirt up ahead through the trees, veering off to the right. I was gaining, but he was still too far ahead. He was probably only one or two sudden turns away from losing me altogether—I had to act fast.

Catching a glimpse of an opening through the trees, I jerked the bike off the trail and crashed through the underbrush, swerving to avoid exposed roots and boulders that jutted out into my path. I climbed up and up a steep rise, branches and leaves slapping my arms and sticky spiderwebs clinging to my face. From the sound of Max's bike, I could tell I was getting closer, cutting him off at the pass as I'd intended to do. But then I saw the gully ahead.

It was a few feet deep, and I couldn't see any way around it. Not without losing my mark in the process. Only one thing to do.

I took a deep breath and gunned the engine, pointing my wheel straight toward the narrowest part of the gully. At the last possible moment, I yanked up my front wheel and clenched the bike between my legs as I sailed through the air, my stomach doing somersaults all the while.

It was the longest two seconds of my life.

But then it was over, and my bike—not my face, thankfully—hit the ground on the other side of the gully. I stumbled a bit but righted myself quickly and kept riding. I found myself at the top of a rise, looking down at the dirt path running below. Sure enough, I caught sight of Max's red shirt in the distance, flying down the path toward me.

I crouched down into the bushes out of sight, waiting for just the right moment. Then, just when Max was about to ride past me, I tore down the hill at top speed and came to a stop right in front of him.

"*Ahh!*" Max shrieked in surprise. He jerked his bike to the side to avoid a collision and toppled over, the bike pinning his leg to the ground. Max looked up at me, his face a mixture of rage and disbelief.

"I appreciate the scenic tour," I said, getting off my bike and wiping the spiderwebs from my face. In the distance, I could hear the wailing of a police car arriving on the scene. "But I think it's time you come with me."

About an hour later, Joe and I were at the station, giving our statements to the police. Adam Parker had met us there and was currently identifying the stolen items that the officers had retrieved from Max's house.

After we'd finished talking to the police sergeant, he left us in his office to go file his report. Joe was slouched in his chair, holding a can of cold soda against the black eye that was rapidly developing on his face. He caught me staring at him and sniffed. "You should have seen the other guy," he said.

"I *did* see the other guy," I countered. Gavin Cook had been angry when the cops pulled him out of the house, but otherwise unscathed.

Joe huffed. "Yeah, well, he hit me with a dictionary—the punk. Who does that? Anyway, I got him, didn't I?"

"You sure did," I agreed, and as if on cue, the interrogation room door opened, and a familiar voice—Max Kingsley's—rang down the hall.

"Listen!" Max was shouting as the officers led him and Gavin back to the cells. "I keep telling you—we stole the stuff, okay? I admit it. But the back door was unlocked; the house was practically inviting us in! And we didn't assault anybody or play any pranks! We were only in that house *once*, I swear—the day before the estate sale. You've got to believe me, man!"

"Uh-huh," I heard the officer mutter.

"Look, they got their stuff back, okay?" Max was pleading. "No harm, no foul, right? Nobody got hurt!"

"Tell it to the judge, kid," the officer said, and closed the door to the cells behind him.

Joe leaned back in his chair, popped open his can of soda, and took a long swig. "Well!" he said, smacking his lips. "Looks like another job well done by the Hardy brothers! I guess you were right, Frank. No ghosts this time—just a couple of superfans with criminal tendencies."

"What about Peter Huang?" I asked. "Could those two have still been working with Peter? Maybe they took care of the stealing and he did the rest?"

Joe thought about it and sighed. "I don't know, Frank. Maybe I was reaching with all that stuff Peter said. If he was in on it, don't you think they would have given him up to the police by now, to save themselves?"

I shrugged. "Maybe. But if Peter had something on them—blackmail or some other kind of threat—then they might not be so eager to throw him under the bus right away." I paused, mulling it over. "Although it would be easier to believe that they're just lying, and really did do the whole thing themselves."

"Occam's razor," Joe added, referencing the idea that the simplest explanation is usually the one that's true.

"Okay," I said, putting my hands up in mock surrender. "For now, let's assume that we've done our job and the case is solved. I'm sure the police will keep questioning them—maybe a night in lockup will loosen their tongues a bit."

Just then the sergeant poked his head back into the office. "All right, gentlemen," he said. "You're all set. Thank you for your statements—we'll be in touch if we need anything else." He shook hands with Joe and me, and we left the room. On the way out, we passed by the evidence room, where Adam Parker was still filling out paperwork with a young officer.

"Hey, Hardy brothers!" Adam called, waving us in.

We walked into the plain white room, which held a large table in front, and row upon row of shelves in back, each one piled with bulging brown paper bags and white filing boxes. The contents of one box, which included what looked like several first-edition copies of Nathan Foxwood's books, a man's wristwatch, and some other items, were arranged on the table, each one sporting a yellow label or tag.

"Guys, I don't know what to say," Adam said when we approached. He was wearing one of his trademark bow ties—this one was green and covered in tiny mustaches. It was fascinating. I wondered what his closet looked like. "Thank you so much. I can't believe how quickly you two managed to catch the perpetrators!"

"Yeah," I said, still feeling a little uncomfortable with the idea that the case was solved. It just felt too . . . easy. "I can't believe it either."

"No problem at all," Joe said smoothly, and stepped in a little closer to Adam. "And if you could, uh, just put in a good word with Mrs. Foxwood, I would absolutely *love* to get my hands on one of those first editions. You know, if she was wondering what type of thank-you gift I'd like . . ."

Adam chuckled. "Sure thing, Joe," he replied. He blew out his cheeks, a look of relief on his face. "You know," he said thoughtfully, "the only people who are going to be upset about this arrest are the press! They were so excited about this whole Gray Hunter ghost story—they're going to be pretty disappointed when they find out it was just two troublesome teenagers behind the whole mess."

Yeah, I thought. *So will Peter Huang. All his beloved hype will be—poof!—gone. Will Nathan Foxwood fade back into obscurity before Peter can get one last bestseller out of him?*

"I'm sure they'll get over it," Joe said. A moment later his eyebrow quirked up in thought. "Hmm, maybe I should give Aisha a call. I bet she'd love to have an exclusive with the guy who caught these two thieves red-handed. . . ."

I rolled my eyes.

"Well my friends, I'm off," Adam announced. "I've got some things to take care of over at the manor tonight. Maybe now that this is all over, I'll finally have time to start writing that book of my own. Let's make a plan to see each other soon—and thanks again!" With that, he walked out of the room with a spring in his step.

The young officer began loading the evidence back into

the box, which was labeled FOXWOOD CASE #051517. "Adam doesn't get to take those things back with him?" I asked.

"Not yet," the officer replied. "Not until after the judicial process is finished. For now, it will just sit in this room with all the other Foxwood evidence. It seems like we've been building quite a collection lately."

"You mean all the stuff from Mr. Foxwood's accident?" I said.

"Nasty business, that accident," the officer muttered.

My ears perked up. "Were you on the scene that night?" I asked.

He grimaced. "Yeah, I was there," he said. "The car was an almost unrecognizable wreck at the bottom of the cliff near the house. The gasoline in the tank must have ignited when it hit the ground—it was still smoldering when we got there hours after the fact. And as far as Mr. Foxwood . . . well, there wasn't much left of the guy. Just a bunch of blackened bones and rags, really. Pretty gruesome—though I've seen worse."

"That fire must have burned pretty hot," Joe said.

The officer shrugged. "Must have. I mean, it probably burned all night! No one knew it had happened until the next day, because the manor is so out of the way, and no one else was home except Mr. Foxwood. And it was plenty hot, believe me."

Joe glanced over at me. I saw a look of uncertainty pass over his face, but he quickly shook it away, like a buzzing fly.

"How was Mr. Foxwood's body identified then?" I asked. "Dental records?"

"No need," the officer replied. "It was his car, the tracks led straight from the manor to the cliff side, and we found his wedding ring on the body. And anyway, his wife had seen him earlier that day and confirmed that he'd been acting very irrationally, which was why she left, for her own safety. The guy was clearly off his rocker and just drove off the cliff—I mean, it's no wonder. Have you read his books?" The officer gave an exaggerated shiver. "Ugh, creepy stuff. Probably drive anyone out of his mind. Anyway, there was just nothing to investigate—it was an open-and-shut case. Mrs. Foxwood wasn't interested in a deeper inquiry—she just seemed to want to put the whole awful mess behind her."

"I can understand that," I said.

The officer pushed a lid onto the box, slid it up onto a shelf with the other evidence, and ushered us out of the room.

Joe and I walked out of the coffee-scented police station and onto the sidewalk in downtown Bayport. It was dusk, and the sun was setting in a riot of pink and orange clouds. The air was warm for a change, and the street was bustling with people. It was a perfectly nice day, and we had just solved another mystery. I should have been on top of the world.

So why did I feel like we had missed something?

THE HUNTER STRIKES AGAIN

9

JOE

IN THE DREAM I WAS AT THE BEACH ON A WARM, sunny day. The sand was white and soft, and the ocean was a perfect, clear blue. Aisha was there. She was in the middle of telling me that I was a hero, and that she was going to feature me on the front page of the newspaper, when suddenly I was attacked by a huge, buzzing swarm of bees.

Nothing like having a nice dream and then ending up covered in bees.

"*Ah!*" I woke up with a start, slapping my face and body all over to repel the imaginary insects that plagued me. After a second I realized I'd just been dreaming, but for some reason I could still hear the buzzing. I turned over to see my cell phone buzzing itself silly on top of my nightstand. It was an unknown number. My clock read 5:20 a.m.

"Do you know what time it is?" I croaked into the phone after accepting the call.

"No," a familiar voice croaked back. "I have a concussion."

"Adam?" I said, sitting up in bed. "Is that you? Where are you? What's going on?"

"I'll answer your questions in order," the voice replied. "Yes; at the hospital; and I took a swan dive into a side table after being chased by some kind of evil poltergeist. Possibly. The jury is still out."

I jumped out of bed. "What? You mean in the manor? Someone attacked you?"

"It's okay, I'm *fine*," he said, his voice slurring a little. "I mean, my head is totally not fine, but the doctors said I'll be up on my feet again in a couple days. Right now I feel a little . . . funny."

"Listen, don't move—Frank and I are coming to see you."

Adam chuckled. "Oh, I can't *move*, Joe! I've got all these tubes attached to me. If I moved, what would happen to the tubes?"

Oh boy. The guy got a bump on the head, all right.

"Listen," Adam continued, obviously trying to focus. "The press got wind of what happened to me and are going wild about it. They'd dropped the whole ghost story angle after those two boys were arrested, but now that there's been another attack with those two out of the picture, they're all excited again. There might be a mob of reporters outside when you get here, so just tell the doctors who you are, and they'll let you in to see me."

"Okay, Adam," I replied. "Be there soon."

I hung up the phone and ran to Frank's room, shaking him out of sleep.

"Wha? Hey, Joe—quit it!" he protested. "Man, the sun isn't even up! What do you want?"

"Adam Parker just called me," I told him. "He's in the hospital. Says someone—or something—attacked him in Cliffside Manor last night. It's not over, Frank."

Upon hearing this, Frank stood up quickly, his fists clenched. "I knew it! I knew something wasn't right! Max Kingsley was telling the truth—they weren't the ones playing at being the Gray Hunter and frightening people. Someone else is behind this—maybe we were on the right track with Peter Huang and Edwin Queen. But why attack Adam? Why now?"

I shook my head. "I don't know. Let's go talk to him—he might be able to shed some light on the situation."

After pushing through half a dozen reporters stationed in the hospital lobby, waiting to talk to Adam, we walked into his hospital room about an hour later and found him watching some kind of nature show about bears. He had gauze wrapped around one side of his head and was dressed in a hospital gown, but he may as well have been naked without his bow tie on. Poor guy. "Hey, you made it," he said when we walked in. "Check it out—bears. I love bears."

Frank and I exchanged a meaningful look. "Hey, Adam," I said cheerfully. "We brought you some ice cream." Frank had protested the stop at the corner store for some medicinal dairy products, but I'd insisted. If anything can bring a man back to himself after a traumatic experience, it's ice cream.

I handed the carton over to him with a plastic spoon, and he took it gratefully. "Oh, thanks, man. Peanut butter cup! My favorite!" He popped open the lid and shoveled several large spoonfuls into his mouth, closing his eyes as he ate. When he opened them again a minute later, he seemed a little more focused than before.

"I really needed that," he finally said with a sigh. "It's been a crazy night. Those reporters are really clawing at the door! I guess I'll have to talk to them eventually. But you guys get the scoop first. I'll tell you everything I can remember."

I elbowed Frank in the stomach. *"See?"* I whispered. *"Ice cream!"*

Adam steepled his fingers in front of his face and furrowed his brows in concentration. "Let me see," he murmured. "So after I left you guys at the police station, I headed straight over to the manor—it was dusk, so that must have been around six o'clock. I ended up going through all the papers from the estate sale and sorting some of Mr. Foxwood's manuscripts—all in boxes in the second-floor study—for historic preservation. It took a while, longer than I'd anticipated. By the time I finished up it was late, almost midnight.

I was about to go get a glass of water from the kitchen when I was startled by this loud noise—like a splintering crash. I froze, and after a few seconds I heard it again. And again. Every few seconds. I thought maybe some kind of animal, like a raccoon or something, had gotten into the house. So I picked up a poker from the fireplace in the office and crept out into the hallway. It was dark—that house gets real dark at night, never had enough modern lighting installed. The sound was coming from a room at the end of the hallway, an old bedroom that the Foxwoods had never used. The door was ajar. When I looked in, I saw a man standing in front of the mantelpiece, hacking at an oil painting on the wall with an ax. But this was no ordinary man. He was"—Adam paused—"glowing. With this weird, bluish light. He was tall and broad, and wore these strange gray clothes and black boots, like something from another time. I looked at the painting that he was destroying and saw that it was a portrait of the man who'd built Cliffside Manor, the one that the Gray Hunter supposedly killed in that old story."

Adam stopped for a moment and shook his head, as if he himself couldn't believe the things he was telling us he saw. "I must have made a noise," he continued. "A gasp, something—because the man stopped what he was doing and turned around. His eyes were like black, empty holes in his head, and when he spoke, it was as if his voice was somehow amplified all around the room. Like it was everywhere at once. He said, 'They took my land from me. And now they're dead. Is that what you want too?' He started to advance toward me, the ax at the ready—and I panicked. I backpedaled out of the room and turned to run back down the hall, but there was a wrinkle in the carpet and I stumbled and fell. My head smashed into the corner of a table and I blacked out. I'm not sure how long I was out, but when I came to, I had just enough wits about me to pull out my phone and call an ambulance." Adam sighed and rubbed his temples. "Anyway, that's it. Believe it or not, that's what happened."

Frank was slumped over in his chair, rubbing his chin thoughtfully. "Well," he finally said. "Max Kingsley and Gavin Cook were in jail overnight, so clearly they couldn't be the ones who attacked you. So now we have to investigate the possibility that they weren't working alone. Let me give the police a call real quick." He pulled out his phone and dialed the local police station, asking to speak with the officer who had interviewed us yesterday. After a short conversation, he hung up, shaking his head. "Officer Webb says that Max and Gavin have sworn up and down that not only were they not working with anyone else, they have no idea who this 'Gray Hunter' could be. Apparently"—here Frank rolled his eyes—"they think that it really is a ghost. They told the police that that's who killed Nathan Foxwood. Ran him off the road." Frank looked at me with an expression that dared me to agree with them.

I threw my hands up in surrender. "Hey, look, bro, I'm

not going to argue with you. It's probably not a real ghost. But right now we don't have a good explanation for all this glowing-guy-with-a-hatchet stuff, so until we come up with one, we've got to at least try and play by his rules."

Frank crossed his arms. "Okay, I'll bite. So what are the rules?"

"Well," I said with relish, "if this was one of Nathan Foxwood's books or movies, then the heroes—that would be you and me, Frank—would naturally then decide that the only way to find out more about the ghost would be to stay in the haunted house. Overnight."

I watched as the color drained from my brother's face. "Oh," he said.

"If there aren't really any bloodthirsty apparitions, as you say," I added, "then we've got nothing to worry about, right?"

"Unless it's actually just a bloodthirsty murderer instead," Frank argued. "You know, a live one?"

"Hmm, true," I said. "But listen—I've got a great idea. Whether it's Peter Huang or Edwin Queen or someone else entirely behind this, it seems like at least part of their motive is to make a scene—create drama surrounding the manor. So if we feed into that—give my reporter friend a heads-up that we're staying in the house overnight, for instance—they'll be unable to resist using the opportunity for their own gain."

Frank eyed me with suspicion. "So, you want us to be bait. In a ghost trap."

I shrugged. "Yeah, kind of. You got a better idea?"

Frank sighed. "Fine," he said. "We'll stay in the house. But I'm not going to like it."

"That's okay," I said, grinning. "I'll like it enough for both of us."

Adam had been looking back and forth between us as we bickered like he was watching a tennis match. When he saw that we were done, he fished inside a backpack next to his bed and pulled out an old-fashioned gold key. "Well, here's the key to the manor," he said, handing it to me. "Good luck. And hey—" He reached out and grabbed my wrist as I got up to leave. "Be careful in there. I don't want you guys to end up in a bed here with me. Or worse."

I swallowed, a little twinge of fear creeping into my armor of easy confidence. "We'll be careful," I said.

I looked at my watch. It was seven a.m. In about twelve hours, Frank and I would be stepping into the scariest place this side of the Mississippi—alone. What would we find there?

Or rather . . . what would find us?

A GHOSTLY MESSAGE

10

FRANK

THERE WAS A BLOODY SUNSET ON THE horizon when Joe and I once again pulled through the gates of Cliffside Manor. On the air was the scent of burning wood; normally a comforting smell, but it carried with it a bad omen. There was not another house for miles, and this one was empty. If there was a fire, who had set it?

I pulled my pack from the trunk. It was heavy with gear—flashlights, energy bars, spare batteries, canisters of water—all the necessities for a night spent in a house of unknowns. Joe's bag was much lighter. I'd watched him pack it. It contained exactly three items: his phone charger, a Coke, and a regulation baseball bat. I had to hand it to Joe: when it came down to business, he always liked to keep it simple.

Joe pulled out the key Adam had given us and unlocked the front door. It opened with a creak, a sound like the whining growl of a cat about to pounce. We stepped inside the front room. It was murky and full of shadows. Most of the windows were covered in heavy velvet drapes that were probably older than I am. I took out my flashlight and switched it on, shining it around the room. Assorted pieces of furniture and decor sat around, each festooned with a yellow SOLD! label. *They must still be waiting for pickup after the sale*, I thought.

Outside, the rumble of distant thunder promised a less-than-quiet evening. I hunched my shoulders and shivered.

"You okay, bro?" Joe asked me.

"Yeah," I said quickly, straightening up. "I'm fine, it's just really cold in here." And it was. Sure, I might also be a little freaked out by the prospect of spending the night in this nightmare factory, but it didn't help that it was practically subzero temperatures in there. Obviously the furnace wasn't on, and the old place retained heat about as well as a fishing net. "We need to find a room upstairs with a fireplace," I said, thinking about the smell of smoke from outside. "We'll freeze in here tonight if we don't get a fire started. And blankets. We need blankets."

"Death by lack of blankets," Joe mused as we made our way up the staircase. "Yeah, not a good look."

On the second floor, we managed to find a smallish bedroom with two twin-size beds and a clean fireplace already set up with logs and kindling. I dropped off my bag on one of the beds and started rooting through it to find some matches. After emptying the entire thing, I tossed it back down in annoyance. "I could have sworn I packed those matchboxes!" I muttered. "Ah, well, I'll just have to go look for some. There's probably a bunch in the kitchen. I'll be right back."

"Hey!" Joe protested. "Don't say that!"

I stopped in my tracks and turned around. "What?"

"We are alone in a haunted house, and you just said, 'I'll be right back,'" Joe answered. "Haven't you ever seen a horror movie?"

I blinked.

Joe rolled his eyes. "When people say that they'll be right back, then they *never come back, man.*"

I stared at my brother for a full minute before saying, "Okay . . . then, I *won't* be right back?"

"God, you're hopeless," Joe said, throwing up his hands.

I shrugged and left the room. What did he want from me, anyway?

After walking back downstairs, I noticed that a few books had fallen to the floor beside a bookshelf. Unable to stop myself from cleaning up the mess, and I perused their covers while I set them back on the shelf. I had just set the last one back in its place when I heard a strange, tinkling sound coming from somewhere nearby. I was certain it hadn't been there when we walked in, so what could it be? With the beam of my flashlight lighting the way, I followed the sound down the hallway to Mr. Foxwood's study. Now that I was closer, I recognized what it was—the song of a music box. Sure enough, when I walked through the door into the study, the first thing I saw was a little child's music box sitting open on Mr. Foxwood's writing desk. It was yellowed with age, and the gold paint around its scalloped edges had chipped off in spots. The inside of it was moldering pink velvet, and a slender ballerina perched there, spinning erratically to the sound of the music.

It would have been pretty if her head wasn't missing.

I reached out and slammed the box shut. My hand was shaking as it rested on the lid.

The room was silent again. I couldn't decide if that was worse or better than it was with the creepy-sweet music playing.

One thought kept running through my mind. That music box couldn't have wound itself. Someone had opened it. Someone was in the house.

I spun and shone the flashlight around the room until I found a floor lamp and quickly switched it on. It flooded the room with warm yellow light, and I scanned every corner for an intruder. But no one was there.

I closed my eyes, commanding my wildly beating heart to slow down. *Whoever is doing this,* I told myself, *they're doing these stunts to throw us off the scent. To scare us. Focus, Frank. Focus on the facts!*

I took several deep breaths and felt a measure of calm return to me. When I opened my eyes again, I found myself staring straight at the reason that I'd come down here in the first place: a box of matches. I stuffed them in my pocket and was about to go back upstairs when I realized that we'd also need some kindling for the fire. Spying a wastebasket next to the writing desk, I knelt down next to it and started pulling out a bunch of crumpled papers. Mostly old bills, from what I could tell, many of them overdue. One of the papers, though, was a letter. Curious, I smoothed it out and saw that it was from Mr. Foxwood's editor, dated about a month and a half ago. It just looked like a regular message, nothing official. *Hadn't these guys ever heard of e-mail?* I wondered. Then I remembered what I'd read about Mr. Foxwood being quirky and old-fashioned, and it made more sense. It was true, I realized. In the whole house I'd never seen evidence of a TV or a computer anywhere. The letter read:

> *Dear Nathan,*
>
> *I hope this letter finds you well. I'm very interested to see your completed draft of* The Haunting of Cliffside Manor—*I admit I am a bit confused as to why you've refused to share any of the partial manuscript with me, as you have in the past. I know you already feel considerable pressure for this book to sell, given what happened with* The Village of Ash, *and I am sorry to add to it, but I must*

tell you that if we don't get a substantial return on investment with this latest novel, I'm afraid I won't be able to convince Steve Lane and the rest of the team to renew your contract. The sales of your backlist titles have been declining for more than five years now, and some of those will likely go out of print in the near future. Unfortunately, the Foxwood brand just doesn't have the power that it used to, and as a company, we'll have to move on if it doesn't recover. At any rate, please let me know when you have a draft ready for review.

I'm doing my best for you, Nathan. I hope you believe that.

Your friend and editor,

Michael Hammer

As I finished reading the letter, I could feel the gears in my head turning, taking in this new information. So not only had Nathan Foxwood's career been in major decline, as Joe had found out, if this newest book didn't hit the bestseller list, his decorated, long-lasting career as a novelist would actually be over. That could certainly account for the guy's unbalanced state of mind prior to his death.

Suddenly I began to wonder—had this crime begun not after Nathan Foxwood's death, but before? As Mr. Foxwood's agent, Peter Huang would have known about the warning letter. He would have known that it would be just as bad for his bottom line as it would have been for Mr. Foxwood's. He'd said that Nathan was worth more dead than alive, so was it possible that he was desperate enough to make that thought a reality? Or was his death just a convenient happenstance, and Peter took the opportunity to take advantage of it for his own gain? Either way, Peter had motive. And he knew Mr. Foxwood's books better than anyone—knew the contents of his new novel too, so he would have been able to put together a very convincing Gray Ghost costume if need be.

There was still the problem of Peter being at the memorial when the figure in the house appeared, but there had to be a way around that. Peter could have paid someone off to do it and then disappear. Anything was possible.

I had to get back to Joe and let him know. I stuck the letter into my pocket with the matchbox and gathered up the rest of the papers from the wastebasket in my arms for kindling. Standing up, I found myself in front of the old typewriter, where I had first read a portion of Mr. Foxwood's story at the estate sale. There was still a piece of paper rolled into the typewriter, but right away I could tell it was different from the one I'd seen before. That one had several paragraphs written on it, but this had only a few words. As I read the message written there, my heart, in defiance of my earlier command, started beating rapidly once again.

GET OUT, HARDY BOYS, it read. *WHILE YOU STILL CAN.*

GET OUT 11

JOE

WHILE FRANK WAS WANDERING around downstairs, hopefully not being murdered by poltergeists, I was pacing the cold bedroom, eating my feelings.

I was on my third energy bar when I realized we had only brought four energy bars, and two of them were supposed to be for Frank. I threw the wrappers in the fireplace and scolded myself for being so jumpy. After all, hadn't I always thought it would be amazing to be in a big old house like this at night, just like in my favorite Foxwood novel? Aside from my dad being a private detective, part of the reason I'd fallen in love with solving mysteries was because of those books. And now, here I was, living the dream!

The problem was, a lot of dreams seem great in your head, but in reality—they are actually super terrifying.

I wrapped my arms around myself and shivered. It was bone-chillingly cold in this house. What was taking Frank so long finding those matches? If it had been me going, I probably would have planned some crazy prank to scare him on my way back, but this was Frank we were talking about. Frank's idea of a crazy prank would be to swap our toothbrushes and see if I noticed.

Suddenly I began to hear the tapping of raindrops on the roof, slow at first, but then picking up speed, until they became a steady drumbeat above my head. I pulled the gauzy curtain aside and peered out the window at the downpour outside, which had transformed the world into a dark smear of shadows, highlighted every few seconds by a flash of distant lightning. It was a picture-perfect backdrop to one of those nail-biting thrillers I loved so much.

And then, as if the universe was saying, *You ain't seen nothin' yet*, a crash of thunder was quickly followed by the bedside lamp going out.

I shuffled over to the lamp and flicked the switch a couple of times, but to no avail. After trying both of the other two lamps in the room and finding them unresponsive, I figured that the storm must have knocked out power to the house.

"Cool," I muttered into the gloom. "Cool, cool, cool . . ."

Be careful what you wish for, I thought grimly. *You just might get it.*

I groped around on the floor until I hit on the backpacks. I knew Frank had brought another flashlight along, so I began pulling items out of his bag, feeling around for the cold metal cylinder. As I searched, I heard the creak of the door opening behind me.

"Oh, Frank," I said, without turning around. "Good timing. Looks like we lost power. I'm trying to find a flashlight, but of course it's lost in this mountain of stuff you brought . . . are these books? You brought *books* to a haunted house? When did you think you'd have time to read on this trip? This bag must weigh a ton. . . ."

Frank said nothing.

"Anyway, did you find the matches? You've been gone forever. I thought you'd been eaten by the Ghost of Christmas Future or whatever. It's cold in here. How are we supposed to solve this case if I can't even feel my fingers?"

Again, Frank said nothing.

"Jeez, Frank—is this a backpack or a black hole? I can't find anything in here. Did you take both flashlights with yo—Oh, my phone, duh! Watching me struggle like this is not funny, Frank." I turned to peer through the darkness at the open door, expecting to see my brother standing there laughing at me.

But what I saw instead made me forget all about the phone and flashlight and reach for the baseball bat.

There in the doorway, illuminated by an otherworldly blue light, was a figure whose face was hidden behind a dark hood. Gripped in his large hands was an ax, its blade glinting in the moonlight.

"Oh," I said, stupidly.

The figure was so still that part of me believed he was just a glow-in-the-dark statue or mannequin that some joker had placed there to freak me out, but then he stepped into the room.

"Joseph Hardy," a voice said. It sounded like a whisper but was so loud that it seemed to be coming from everywhere at once. "You do not belong here."

I swallowed, my throat suddenly dry as a bone. At the end of the day, I didn't believe in ghosts any more than Frank did. I mean, maybe in theory, but not in reality—and not like this. But whoever this was, they were doing a heck of a good impression of one. "Who . . . ," I began, working to get the words out. "Who are you?"

The figure continued to advance on me, slowly, like a thunderstorm, his voice growing in volume as it came. "I am the one who owns this land. I am vengeance, bloody and unmerciful. I am the hunter, and for your crimes, tonight—you will suffer."

After a beat, I said, "Yeah, um . . . I appreciate the offer of, you know, bloody vengeance, but I think this time I'll pass."

"You have no choice," the voice boomed, and I saw his fingers grip the ax tightly. "First you will suffer, and then you will leave this place. Forever." And with those words, the Gray Hunter raised the ax above his head and brought it down with a mighty swing.

My instincts kicking in, I dove backward over the bed behind me, and the blade smashed into the bedpost, splintering it into smithereens. Whether or not the ghost was real, that ax sure was.

Before the Hunter could yank the ax out from the wood, I leaped to my feet and made a beeline for the door. "Get out!" the voice commanded, still seeming to come from every inch of the house. "Get out!"

I tore out of the room, and it wasn't until I was in the hallway that I remembered my bat—still sitting on the floor of the bedroom. I cursed my own foolishness, in allowing panic to keep me from remembering to arm myself. I stole a glance behind me, figuring the Hunter would be giving chase, but the hallway was deserted.

Somehow, that was worse.

Scanning the hallway, I grabbed a brass candlestick from a side table and hefted it in my hand. It wasn't a baseball bat, but it would have to do.

"I'm not leaving until I find out who you really are!" I said into the silence. I ran down the hallway slowly, I needed to get downstairs and find Frank. My pulse was roaring in my ears, and every time the lightning crashed outside and the hallway lit up with a strobe-like light, I had to grit my teeth to keep from shouting out loud.

The darkness was like a stranglehold on my reason, and

even the air smelled of sweat and fear. There was a man in the house who wanted me dead—whether or not he was dead himself didn't seem to matter much anymore.

I had backed almost to the end of the hallway, where I could take the stairs back down to where Frank had gone, when suddenly a whispering voice spoke. But this time, it wasn't coming from everywhere at once. No, it was spoken directly into my ear, so close that I could feel a cold breath blow across my cheek.

It said only one word.

"Suffer."

A moment later I experienced an explosion of pain as something struck me in the back of the head, and everything went black.

When I woke up, my first sensation was delight. *Yay!* I thought. *I'm not dead!* (This may seem like a weird thing to be delighted about, but you'd be surprised how many times I've had a little mental party about that exact same thing. I should have the local bakery make me a cake every time we finish a case. *Congratulations!* it would say in yellow icing. *You Didn't Die!*)

But my jubilation was short-lived, because I quickly realized that, along with having a raging headache, I was being dragged by the ankles down a different hallway by a gigantic glowing man.

"Why . . . ?" I murmured, still groggy from the head

bonking. "Why are you doing this?" It was the one big question mark I had about this whole thing. Why would anyone haunt the house of a dead writer?

"I killed the man who built this house, long ago," the figure said, his voice unnaturally amplified once again. "People stayed away for a long time. But then they forgot. They forgot me, they forgot that this is my land. And when the new people came, I punished them as well. Now they, too, are gone."

The figure stopped in front of a doorway; the room inside was pitch black. With one effortless heave, he tossed me inside. I groaned as my head jerked painfully back and hit the floor. I lifted my head slightly, squinting at the bluish nimbus of light that seemed to surround the Hunter's whole body. All except his face, which was still completely hidden under his black hood. "I am making sure," the Hunter said with finality, "that people will not forget again."

He slammed the door, and my world was once again only darkness.

12 NOT AFRAID

FRANK

ABOUT A MINUTE AFTER SEEING THE threatening note on the typewriter, all the lights in the house went out. It startled me, and I dropped the flashlight. Yikes, this whole thing had me on edge. I picked up the flashlight, but it seemed that the drop put it out of commission. I sighed and pulled the box of matches out of my pocket and lit one. The light it cast was pitiful against the wall of darkness in the house, but it was better than nothing. I groped my way back out of the room and into the hallway, bumping into furniture as I went. Outside, a storm had begun, and occasional lightning strikes illuminated the house with bursts of white light.

Suddenly the silent house was full of strange noises coming from the second floor. A sound like a loud voice trickled down to where I was standing. But it was too muffled to understand what it was saying. Could it be Joe calling down to me? I supposed I had been gone for a while. He might be worried that I'd been devoured by monsters or something. I was approaching the stairs when the voice was replaced by something else—the sound of something large and heavy being dragged across a floor.

Something like a body.

"Joe!" I shouted, my heart starting to race.

I was about to take the stairs two at a time when I heard a door slam. I froze in place, hoping against hope that Joe would appear on the landing, flashlight in hand, to tell me that he had just been dragging an unattractive area rug to another room. Or a sack of hammers. Or a bear.

No luck.

The figure that emerged silently from the hallway was tall and broad, with a black hood hiding his face and an ax hanging by his side. It was the same figure I'd seen, only for a moment, outside the window at the estate sale. But this time, his mere presence wasn't the strangest thing about him—no, that had to be the fact that he was glowing.

It was the eerie, bluish glow that Adam had described. It emanated from his entire body—even the ax.

There, in that dark and empty house, with forks of lightning framed in the dusty windows, the sight of this apparition was like something out of a movie. My eyes did not want to believe what they were seeing. And yet, there he was. The Gray Hunter.

No.

I closed my eyes, blocking out the world for a moment, and allowed the voice of reason the opportunity to speak.

This is not real. This is what he wants, the voice said. *To create an image so terrifying that it shuts out every other thought. To frighten people and drive them away from this place, so that they can go and tell reporters what they saw here. So that Nathan Foxwood's name will forever be spoken with a whisper of awe and terror. So it will never be forgotten.*

And Peter Huang could make a fortune.

I knew I was close to the answer—but somehow, it still didn't feel right. Didn't ring true. Again, I was missing something. Something big.

But there was something much more important than that at stake right now.

"If you've hurt my brother," I said, my voice low and dangerous, "then ghost or not, I will come after you and make you pay."

"Your brother is alive—for now," the Gray Hunter said, his voice coming not from him, but somehow, from everywhere. It was loud, and I could feel it down to the soles of my shoes. "You and he have trespassed on my land for the last time tonight."

"I'm not a fool!" I replied. "I don't believe in ghosts.

Whatever you're trying to accomplish here, you need to stop it right now, before you go too far."

There was a pause, and the Gray Hunter cocked his head and moved closer to the second-floor railing above me. He lifted the ax and pointed the blade in my direction before speaking again.

"You do not need to believe to die."

A moment later I heard a very soft whooshing sound above my head, like a cord unraveling. I looked up, where a large crystal chandelier was hanging. A split second later the room was lit up by another bolt of lightning, and it was only by the grace of that moment that I realized that the chandelier was falling.

The next few seconds seemed to move very slowly. With every bit of my strength, I threw my body backward from the spot, hitting the cold tile a few feet back and sliding, just as fifty pounds of metal and glass slammed into the floor where I had been standing. The explosive noise of its impact was immense, and I quickly covered my head with my hands as millions of shards of crystal flew through the air and fell like tinkling rain.

I lay there, still and breathing slowly, until the rain stopped. And when I finally opened my eyes and looked up, the Gray Hunter was standing before me. He reached down with one arm and grabbed me by the collar of my coat, hoisting me to my feet with seemingly little effort. I hung from his grip, my gaze trying unsuccessfully to penetrate the darkness under that hood, to see the face beneath.

"I am giving you and your brother one last chance to leave this place," he said, the voice all around me. "What do you choose? Escape? Or death?"

This is not real, the voice in my head reminded me.

I took a deep breath.

"I choose neither," I said. Then I wound up and punched that would-be ghost right in the face.

I guess Mr. Glow Stick wasn't expecting that, because he stumbled backward with the blow, letting me go in the process. I dropped into a crouch, prepared for him to strike back. But something on my coat caught my eye. It was a smear of blue across the collar, a substance that glowed eerily in the darkness.

And just like that, in a matter of moments, all the many pieces of the puzzle fell into place.

It was the simplest, and yet the most impossible answer. And now I had it.

The Gray Hunter pulled himself up to his full height again and loomed over me, blocking out what little moonlight streamed from the window behind him.

"You have sealed your doom, Frank Hardy," he said.

"You are a kind of ghost, Gray Hunter," I replied. "But I'm not afraid of you. It's your doom that has been sealed. Because I know who you really are."

RED-HANDED 13

JOE

ON ONE HAND, THE FACT THAT IT WAS dark was nice, considering the raging headache I had. On the other hand, being locked in a dark room by a potentially homicidal maniac-slash-ghost was less than thrilling. I had to get out of that room. For all I knew, the Human Glow Stick had left me here so he could go find Frank and bonk him on the head too. Or worse.

I lurched to my feet, disoriented both from the darkness and the minor concussion. I groped ahead of me with both hands, taking small, tentative steps. All I needed was to trip over an ottoman and break my neck—not the way I wanted to go. FAMED YOUNG DETECTIVE FELLED BY UPHOLSTERY just didn't appeal to me as a headline. Eventually I found the wall and crab-walked my way across it until I found the door. Naturally, it was locked, but I gave it a few rattles and kicks anyway. It was an old house, there was a chance that the knob was rickety . . . but no. I was locked in tight. I had to find another way out.

I continued feeling my way across the wall and around a corner, where I felt the leather bindings of books on a shelf and the uneven surfaces of oil paintings, until I reached another corner. What I felt next made my heart leap with hope: thick, velvety fabric. Curtains. And where there were curtains, there must be windows.

I grabbed a fistful of fabric and threw it aside, revealing— thank goodness—a large picture window behind it. The moonlight illuminated the dark room, and I blinked, my eyes adjusting to even that dim light. Within seconds, I had the window unlatched. A blast of wind and rain hit my face as I threw it open, and I stumbled back from the force of it. Shielding my face with my hand, I stuck my head outside to have a look around. First I looked straight down, a drop of at least fifteen feet, and confirmed what I'd already suspected: jumping or climbing down to the ground was out of the question. But this particular window led out onto a very narrow ledge, which stretched back to the middle of the house, where a stone patio jutted out. If only I could reach that patio, I was certain I could break the window with something and reenter the house from there.

There were advantages and disadvantages to this plan.

The disadvantages included the extreme narrowness of the ledge, the slipperiness of said ledge due to the rain, the darkness, the wind, and the clear and present danger of falling fifteen feet onto the concrete below. The advantages were fewer. Well, okay—there was *one* advantage. There was no other plan. This was the only plan, the only way out, and therefore I was going to have to do it.

I took a deep breath and shrugged. "Well," I muttered to myself, "here goes nothing."

I grabbed the window frame and carefully hoisted my body out onto the ledge. In an instant, I was soaked through. I wiped the rain off my face and squinted into the downpour, trying to get my bearings, the clatter of rain pounding on the metal roof filling the world with noise. I started to slide along the ledge, my back pressed up against the house. Pointy bits of brick and stonework poked into me painfully, but I didn't dare lean forward away from them, for fear of losing my balance and toppling off the edge.

I was halfway there—there were probably only six or seven feet left between me and the stone railing of the patio, but it felt miles away. My nose itched. I had a toe cramp. I was maybe going to sneeze. I commanded my brain to focus, to block out everything except reaching that goal, and kept inching along.

Five feet, four, three . . .

And then the sky went white. A bolt of lightning struck so close to the house that I could feel the hair on my arms rise and sizzle with electricity. I had about one or two seconds to realize what was going to happen next before it did.

BOOM!

The thunderclap was so ferociously loud that it took my breath away. Even though I knew how vital it was for me to stand completely still, to make no sudden movements, I couldn't help it—I jumped. And when my feet came back down on that rain-soaked ledge, one held firm, and the other did not. I lurched sideways and felt myself start to fall.

My martial arts training—which, FYI, includes a lot of pretty intense hip-swivel action—kicked in, and I whipped my body back up, reaching out for something to hold on to. My fingernails scraped against the brickwork, cutting my fingers to shreds, but I found purchase on a small stone outcropping and held on for dear life. Using the momentum I already had, I swung myself back up onto the ledge and stood there, panting, my heart pounding like a jackhammer.

Compared to the near-death experience I'd just had, shuffling through the last three feet to the patio was a cinch. I collapsed onto the stone floor and finally scratched my nose. Sweet, sweet relief!

But I didn't have time to celebrate. I had to get to Frank! I ran up to the large picture window and peeked inside. The window looked onto the second-floor landing, where through the open railing, I had a view of the grand entranceway below. There I could see the glowing blue figure of the Gray Hunter pacing the room like a boxer, his fists raised for a fight. In front of him I dimly saw another, smaller figure: Frank. I was flooded with relief to see him alive and well. All around them, the floor glittered as if it were carpeted in diamonds, and nearby I saw the carcass of a chandelier lying broken on the floor.

Man, what had I missed? I was about to try and test the window to see if it was locked when I caught sight of another person, standing just out of the shadows in front of me on the landing. It was too dark for me to make out who it was, but then the sky was once again illuminated by a flash of lightning, and the figure's identity was revealed.

I almost stumbled back in shock. Could it be? Was it really possible?

Everything suddenly made sense. And for the first time that night, I wasn't jumpy or anxious—I felt like Joe Hardy again. In other words: awesome.

Finding the window unlocked—lucky me—I slid it open as quietly as I could and slipped inside the house. The woman in the shadows was so focused on what was going on below, she didn't hear me approach, didn't even hear the drip-drip of my sodden clothing leaking onto the hardwood floor. So she was very surprised when I walked right up next to her and said:

"Hello, Mrs. Foxwood—fancy meeting you here."

Heather Foxwood nearly leaped straight out of her skin, but to her credit, she recovered quickly. She brushed a stray lock of wavy brown hair from her face and regarded me with those piercing blue eyes. For a moment, I could see her nostrils flare and her jaw clench as she recognized my face. But the flash of anger was as fleeting as the lightning and was almost instantly replaced with a doe-eyed, grateful look of relief. "Joe Hardy, is that you? My goodness, you gave me a fright. I'm so glad to see you! I'd heard from Adam that you and your brother were planning to stay in the manor overnight, and I came to warn you. But then the Hunter attacked me, and I was so scared—"

I put a hand up and interrupted her. "Let me stop you right there," I said. "First of all, I have to commend you on a truly remarkable performance. I mean, *bravo*. I'm sure you're a great scientist and everything, but really, you should have considered an acting career."

I could see the panic flooding Mrs. Foxwood's face, but she heroically tried to keep up the ruse. "I don't know what you mean, I—"

"Seriously, it was an amazing plan," I continued. "You sent Frank and me on a pretty brilliant wild-goose chase, and that takes talent. But the lies need to stop."

Suddenly I heard a shout of pain from below, and I whirled to see Frank on his side on the ground, gripping his shoulder with one hand. The Gray Hunter was advancing on him with his ax, and a moment later his booming voice filled the air.

"Time to die, Frank Hardy."

I turned back to the woman in front of me and grabbed

her by the shoulders. "Call off your dead husband, Mrs. Foxwood. Now."

Heather Foxwood looked at me, that anger returning to her face. But it quickly deflated, to be replaced with a look of defeat. "Nathan!" she shouted.

The Gray Hunter, who had his ax raised above his head, froze.

"It's over," Mrs. Foxwood said. "We've got to stop."

He turned around slowly and gazed up at us, where we stood at the railing. He let the ax drop to the floor and pulled the hood from his face, revealing the man I had always seen staring at me from the back covers of my favorite books. His dark beard was longer and unkempt, his hair wilder, but it was, unmistakably, Nathan Foxwood. A dead man walking.

THE GHOSTWRITER 14

FRANK

NORMALLY I WOULD TAKE EVERY opportunity to make fun of my brother, who at the moment was staring at Nathan Foxwood, his eyes wide and his jaw basically on the floor. He and Heather Foxwood had quickly made their way down the stairs as soon as Mr. Foxwood had dropped the ax and removed his hood. But I couldn't muster a jab for Joe—frankly, I understood exactly how he felt. Even though I hadn't been the guy's number one fan, finding out that a dead guy wasn't really dead was quite a shock.

"Well, boys," the deep, booming voice said, echoing around the room. Mr. Foxwood grimaced and reached under his belt, where a small black box was hidden. He pushed a button, and a red light went out. "Well, boys," he repeated, this time in a normal voice, "your dogged persistence seems to have paid off. You've successfully ruined us."

Heather Foxwood walked to her husband's side and folded him into an embrace. "We tried, babe," she told him. "But it was going too far. People were getting hurt."

Nathan Foxwood hung his head. "Yes, I suppose you're right." He looked up again, his green eyes no longer narrowed in anger, but filled with pride. "We never meant for anyone to be injured, merely frightened—you believe me, don't you?"

Joe nodded almost immediately. I hesitated, but then recognized the genuine remorse on both the Foxwoods' faces, and nodded too.

"But the plan was so perfect," Mr. Foxwood went on. "I was *dead*. How did you know?"

Ah, my favorite part of a case! I took a deep breath and was about to launch into a detailed explanation of the myriad clues that led me to my conclusion when my brother opened his big mouth and said, "Well, Mr. Foxwood, sir—and let me just say, I'm a big fan—it wasn't until I saw your lovely wife standing there on the landing just now that it all came together for me."

I rolled my eyes. Leave it to Joe to steal my thunder!

"Seeing Mrs. Foxwood reminded me of when I'd first met her, during the estate sale when this all started. She'd claimed that the Gray Hunter had attacked her at the exact same time that Frank had seen him downstairs, making it seem like he was in two places at once. Obviously, coming from a respected scientist, that meant a lot. But it never occurred to me until a few minutes ago: What if she was lying?" He turned to Mrs. Foxwood. "It was the simplest explanation, but because I automatically believed you, I never even considered it."

Heather Foxwood allowed herself a little smile. "Yes, Joe," she said. "We were counting on that."

"But once I started thinking about you as being in on this, I wondered why you would do it. What was your motivation? And then I remembered something Peter Huang had said, that Nathan Foxwood 'is worth more dead than alive.' He'd been talking about how because Mr. Foxwood was dead and because of all this media hype surrounding the ghost in the manor, his book was going to be a bestseller. And I thought, *Boy, that sounds like a pretty good motive to me.* When I first heard him say it, I immediately became suspicious of Peter himself. After all, he would make a lot of money from a bestseller too!"

"Exactly," I chimed in. "I thought the same thing when I found a letter from your editor in the trash can in your study. It went on and on about how important this last book was, and how you wouldn't get another contract unless *The Haunting of Cliffside Manor* made it big. That was obviously why someone would go to such lengths to pull these crazy stunts. To get attention! Ever since the first sighting of the 'Gray Hunter,' there have been reporters swarming around this place like bees. And why not? It had everything, all the trappings of a great story—the mysterious, sudden death of a writer who just happened to be working on a book about the very haunted house he was living in. Who wouldn't want to read it? It was a recipe for success. Peter had the motive, and ever since those two Foxwood Fan Club members swore that they weren't involved in the hauntings, I was sure Peter was involved somehow. It made sense."

Mr. Foxwood huffed. "Peter is a good agent," he said diplomatically, "but he doesn't have a creative bone in his body."

"Right," Joe said with a grin. "That was the thing. It just didn't sit right with me that the yes-man I saw in that office would have the guts or the imagination to engineer something like this. Who better to do it than the master storyteller himself?"

It was Nathan Foxwood's turn to crack a smile. "It's been a long time since anyone has called me that, son," he murmured.

"It's true," I continued. "It all made sense then—it was your house, your book, your realm of fear and terror: you were the perfect man to have taken on the role of the Gray Hunter and set up all these supposed 'hauntings,' all the while conspiring with your wife, who would make sure everyone on the outside would get the story and all its juicy details."

I paused for a moment. "Except there was one problem.

As you mentioned earlier, you were—very inconveniently—dead. And in my experience, it's very hard for dead people to commit crimes."

"Unless they're zombies," Joe piped up.

"Unless they're zombies," I agreed. "But assuming you weren't a zombie, I needed to figure out how you could be dead, but not dead. And the more I thought about the car accident, the more staged it seemed. It was *your* car, and *your* wedding band inside, but the only remains were some bones—none of which were analyzed by the police, because Mr. Foxwood's distraught wife didn't want an investigation."

I looked meaningfully at Heather Foxwood, who smirked.

"It immediately struck me as odd that after only a handful of hours, all the soft tissue of the body would have been burned away. It takes quite a bit of heat and time to destroy an entire human body—something a scientist like yourself would know very well. Not only that, working in a skeletal research lab would provide you with easy access to bones that could have been planted in the car prior to the crash."

"It was a setup," Joe concluded. "And the two of you controlled every detail of it right from the start. Even putting on a show for Adam Parker's benefit, weeks in advance, to set up your so-called 'deteriorating mental state.' After all, your actions the night of the accident had to make sense—had to fit the story."

"Right," I continued. "And once Mr. Foxwood was

good and dead, he could finally become one of the monsters he'd spent so many years writing about. And since this was your house, you could outfit it with wall-to-wall haunting equipment."

"I'm guessing surround sound throughout the house for the voice," Joe mused. "And hidden passages so you could pop up anywhere you liked without being seen."

Nathan Foxwood nodded. "Correct," he said.

"But the glow . . . ?" Joe asked.

"That's what tipped me off," I said. "When it rubbed off on my hand after I hit you, I suddenly remembered what 'ZnS' stands for. That vat of chemicals I saw in your lab, Mrs. Foxwood, it stuck with me for some reason, and now I know why. It stands for zinc sulfide, a phosphor. If it were mixed with some kind of carrier substance and applied to skin and clothing, it would make them glow. Just like a ghost."

"You guys really are the perfect couple," Joe said, shaking his head in awe.

Heather Foxwood sighed. "It was all going so well until Adam got you guys involved. Of course he meant well; he thought he was helping me in my time of need. So I couldn't tell him to stop without making him suspicious, but I knew you two were trouble."

"That's when I decided to send you on a little wild-goose chase after those two boys," Mr. Foxwood said. "I was leaving the house after putting on that little show for everyone at my memorial service, and I saw you coming after me, Joe.

I figured a little shove might scare you off the trail, and if it didn't, I left behind that little pin to lead you in the right direction. I'd seen that Kingsley boy and his friend break in and steal my things a couple days after the accident—I'd almost stopped them but then thought better of it, thought maybe they'd come in handy. And sure enough, they did."

"Once you tracked them down and got them arrested, we thought we were home free," Heather Foxwood continued. "But then we realized there would be an unforeseen consequence of our plan: the media would lose interest. They'd figure those two boys were behind all the hauntings, too, and so the romance would be gone. The stories would stop running."

Nathan Foxwood nodded. "So we had to start them up again. And when Adam came to the house last night, I knew I had to put on the show for him, so he could go out there and tell people that the Hunter was real after all. But I never meant for him to get hurt." He looked at the floor, his face full of remorse.

Joe rubbed the side of his head and grimaced. "It seems to me you have quite a talent for semi-accidental head injuries," he said. "Did you not mean to hurt Frank and me, either?"

"Things just got out of hand," Mr. Foxwood said. "Our entire plan was on the line—I thought if I could just scare you away, prove to you that the Hunter was real, you would leave us alone. And then the book would come out, my reputation would be restored, we'd be millionaires again, and we could move far away, to a place where no one would recognize my face. A perfect ending."

As if to punctuate the end of Mr. Foxwood's story, the sound of approaching police sirens filled the air, and soon the flash of red and blue lights began illuminating the room through the rain-spattered windows. Joe must have found time to call the police at some point, and it looked like our backup had arrived.

"I'm sorry, Mr. Foxwood, Mrs. Foxwood," I said. "But it seems your story isn't quite over yet."

Nathan Foxwood nodded solemnly and pulled his wife into another tight embrace, looking her straight in the eyes. "We'll get through this, all right? We always do."

She nodded. "At least with you alive again, I won't have to deal with Edwin Queen knocking down my door for a date."

"Queen?" Mr. Foxwood growled, his lip curling in a wolfish snarl. "If that slimeball comes within even ten feet of you, I'll—"

"Shh, sweetheart," Mrs. Foxwood said, putting a finger over his lips. "No threats of violence, please. I think we're in enough trouble as it is."

Mr. Foxwood relaxed and chuckled, then looked back at Joe and me, a measure of respect in his green eyes. "Though I am most displeased that the two of you ruined our plans, I have to say that I'm impressed."

"Thank you," I replied. "And I really am sorry that you were brought to this."

Mr. Foxwood just gave me a sad smile.

I heard the sound of car doors slamming just outside. The police officers would be here any moment now to arrest a dead man and his wife. *That will be quite a story for them to tell their friends tomorrow!* I thought.

Joe was biting his lip and looking like he really wanted to say something, but was afraid to do it.

I sighed and rolled my eyes. "Mr. Foxwood, I know this might seem like an inappropriate request, given the current circumstances," I said. "But can my brother have your autograph?"

A NOVEL IDEA 15

JOE

YOU'D THINK THAT AFTER A NIGHT LIKE that, I'd be too hyped up to sleep, but after we spoke to the police and they went off with the Foxwoods to the station, I was so tired that I collapsed onto the nearest musty old couch and was out like a light.

I didn't wake up again until daylight was streaming into the room. I sat up and rubbed my eyes, feeling a little disoriented. "Frank?" I called out. "Where are you?"

He walked into the room a minute later, chewing on an energy bar and looking pleased with himself. At the sight of the food, my stomach growled in protest. I guess being chased around the house by a ghost/celebrity author really works up an appetite. "Here I am," Frank said.

"Toss me one of those," I said. Frank looked in the bag and shrugged. "Sorry, this was the last one. Here—" He broke the energy bar in half and offered me the larger piece.

"Aw, thanks, bro," I said. As soon as the chocolatey and nutty goodness filled my mouth, I felt a million times better. "So," I said, "where did you end up crashing?"

"In that bedroom where we put our bags, like a normal person," Frank said with a smirk. "Slept like a rock, though. Nothing like that first night after we close a case!" He stretched his arms wide and sighed with contentment.

"I slept really well too," I said. "Maybe they should make this place into a bed-and-breakfast, with optional ghost tours. It would be a gold mine!"

"I don't know . . . ," Frank mused. "I don't think people normally associate comfort and rest with terrifying murder houses."

I shrugged. "Maybe *you* don't, but I would totally stay here for a weekend."

Just then my phone rang. "Hello?"

"So, still alive then, eh?" The familiar voice of local-and-cute reporter Aisha Best filled my head.

"Alive and well," I replied. "And thanks for putting that piece about us staying in the manor last night in the late paper. We cracked the case."

"Really," she said, not bothering to conceal her interest. "How about an exclusive?"

"How about a coffee?" I countered.

"Deal," she said. "Text me the details."

I ended the call and stretched out on the couch again with a contented sigh.

"Do you *have* to date the media, Joe?" Frank asked.

"I don't *have* to," I answered. "But I *want* to."

Frank's orchestra of all-suffering sighs was interrupted by the sound of approaching footsteps. We poked our heads out of the room to see Adam Parker virtually prancing down the hallway toward us. "Hardy brothers!" he exclaimed, smiling from ear to ear. He lifted his fist for a bump and we both obliged.

"Adam, are you okay?" Frank asked. "I thought you'd still be in the hospital. . . ."

"Nah, I'm good, Frank! Got the all-clear a few hours ago. I was just at the police station giving my statement, and I came here straight after to see you guys. I can't thank you enough for everything that you've done."

"Oh, hey—it was our pleasure, man," I replied. "When you were at the station, did you see Mr. Foxwood?"

Adam nodded. "Yeah, they let me in to talk to him. It was so weird . . . I never thought I'd see him again, and there he was—good old Nathan, same as ever."

"Did he say anything about me?" I blurted out, before I could think better of it. Frank covered his eyes and shook his head. I elbowed him.

Adam just smiled. "He *did*, actually. He said that if anyone was going to get him arrested, he was happy that at least it was a couple of very smart young men—one of them a Foxwood superfan to boot."

I beamed.

"All right, all right, don't float away now, Joe," Frank mumbled. "Stay here with us on solid ground."

"Quit pooping on my party, party pooper," I said. "Let me enjoy my moment."

Frank chuckled. "Yeah, okay. Go ahead and enjoy it."

I enjoyed it.

Frank shook his head. "The news is going to be all over this story. Your reporter friend Aisha is going to have a field day when she hears about this."

I nodded. "In a way, they got what they wanted after all. The only difference is, instead of getting famous again, they got *infamous*."

"Does it matter?" Frank said with a shrug. "Those books are going to sell for sure. At least for the moment, Nathan Foxwood is going to be a household name again. Well, we stopped them before things really got out of hand. Now the Foxwoods will have a chance to redeem themselves and use their powers for good instead of evil. It's all over."

There was a pause as we let that sink in. "I can't believe it," I finally said.

"What? That we solved another mystery?" asked Frank.

"No, that my name is going to be printed next to Nathan Foxwood's in the paper." I sighed with contentment. "It's all I've ever wanted."

Frank chuckled and turned to Adam. "So, what's next for you? Are you going back to work with Mr. Foxwood again, now that he's risen from the dead?"

Adam shook his head. "I think I've had enough baby-sitting famous authors for a while. I think it's about time I worked on my own novel."

"Oh, cool," I said. "Do you already have an idea for one?"

Adam brightened and adjusted his bow tie, which was decorated with tiny little quill pens. "Actually, yes," he said. "I think I'm going to write an action-packed mystery. Something exciting, with lots of car chases, explosions, cliff-hangers at the end of every chapter—you know the ones I mean. And the main characters are going to be two amateur detectives, who just happen to be brothers. . . ." He trailed off and waggled his eyebrows at us.

I looked at Frank. We laughed, and I knew I spoke for us both when I added: "Sounds like a bestseller to me!"

FRANK

T'S FUNNY TO THINK ABOUT HAVING ENEMIES.
Not funny ha-ha. Funny strange.

I was standing in line at the First Bayport Bank on Water Street. Dad had sent me here on an errand, explaining that the Hardy household believed in banking in person, not online. Mistakes were less common, he said, when the tellers had a face to remember. Even plain old Frank Hardy's face.

I knew it was just an excuse to get me out of the house. "You're spending too much time cooped up in front of a computer screen." Dad, Mom, Aunt Trudy, and my brother, Joe, each told me that at least five times a day.

Well, they weren't the ones who had to give a speech. That's right: In one week, yours truly had to get up in front of the entire Bayport High School student body to present my American history paper on civil liberties, which my teacher, Ms. Jones, had called "exceptional." I'd been really happy about that until I realized it would lead to mandatory public speaking. Thinking about it gave me turbocharged butterflies. I was embarrassed to admit it, but if there was one thing I truly hated, it was public speaking. D-day was right around the corner, and I didn't even have a final speech yet. I pretended to be "researching," but the reality was that I was turning into Joe: a world-class procrastinator.

The line in the bank was long, and the wait was boring. It had rained all morning, which meant drippy umbrellas inside. My sneakers were soaked through from the walk.

I took out my cell and texted Joe. We were going to meet up later at the Meet Locker to study. (That's a coffee shop, in case you were wondering. A popular hangout, it's open late, and they serve a mean Maximum Mocha.)

NO SIGNAL.

Typical, I thought. Bayport had become notorious for its spotty cell reception.

Staring down at my phone, I accidentally bumped into the person in front of me in line. "Sorry," I said. The guy glanced back. Then, eyes widening, he turned to face me.

It was Seth Diller, Bayport High's very own Quentin Tarantino.

"Oh. Hey, Seth," I said.

He studied me with his strange, unblinking, pale-blue eyes. He looked very highly charged for some reason, like he'd beaten me to the Meet Locker and drunk about twelve espressos. A few inches shorter than me, Seth was wearing a black turtleneck so tight it made me wonder if his brain was being deprived of oxygen. Finally he dipped a nod in my direction. "Frank," he said quietly.

I didn't know Seth very well. But he always had a camera in his hand. He was president of the Bayport High AV Club.

His specialty was monster videos. I'd seen a couple on the club website. Lots of fake tissue damage and gross-out effects. Joe appreciated that Seth took the time to make all his effects "in the camera"—meaning not digitally. No CGI for Seth. He was a purist. Joe was a fan, me not so much.

"Working on any new monster masterpieces?" I asked, just to be friendly.

He nodded. "Yes . . . in fact, I'm cooking up something really special."

"Really?"

He smiled. "That's right. I'm hoping this new movie will break my record of eleven thousand four hundred fifty-six views on YouTube."

I guessed that was impressive. "What's it about?" I asked.

He frowned and gave a shrug. "It's hard to describe."

I figured he didn't want to talk about it, so I just wished him luck and changed the subject. "Hey, how's your brother doing?" Tom Diller, Seth's older brother, had been badly wounded while serving with the marines in Afghanistan.

Seth grew quiet, and I was starting to feel sorry I'd brought up such a personal subject. That's when we heard the screams.

"Everybody stay where you are!" a voice yelled.

Three men with guns, each wearing a mask from a recent slasher movie, had entered the bank. They were moving fast, pistols in their outstretched hands. One disarmed the security guard, dropped the guard's gun in a trash can, and forced him to lie on the floor. Another locked the front doors. The third came toward us.

I'm not going to lie: I was shocked, and a little scared. I could feel my heart hammering in my chest like it was trying to break out. The truth is, I'd been in far stickier situations than this one, but you don't exactly expect to run into a bank robbery on a Saturday morning in a sleepy little town like Bayport.

Seth, standing right beside me, stiffened and made a panicky sound in his throat. Seeing his fear brought me back to my senses. "Stay calm," I whispered to him. "Do whatever they ask. Everything will be fine."

He was fumbling in his pocket. Glancing over, I saw him take out his smartphone. Hands shaking, he hurriedly tapped the screen until a wobbly image of his own feet came up. He had enabled the video cam.

He was going to record the robbery.

"Seth, listen to me very carefully," I said in an urgent whisper. "Do not do that. These men are wearing masks for a reason. Just put your phone away."

But he wasn't listening. He cupped his hand so the phone was partway concealed and held it low against his leg, angling out at the room, capturing the heist in action.

"Empty your pockets and your purses!" the third gunman yelled. He was my height and thin, wearing a bulky army jacket that didn't fit. "Nice and calm, people. No sudden moves. We don't want to hurt anybody."

The gunman who had locked the doors joined him. "But we will shoot anyone who gets in our way!" he shouted. He rushed to one of the tellers' windows and proceeded to collect money from behind the counter.

Army Jacket began taking valuables from the people standing in line. Rings, necklaces, and wallets disappeared into a canvas bag he was carrying. He made quick work of it. My mind was racing. What would be the reaction of the gunmen if they saw Seth recording them? It would depend on a million factors. How experienced they were. How nervous. How desperate. Were these men killers?

Army Jacket reached Seth, standing right by my side. I held my breath. The gunman paused only for an instant while Seth dropped his wallet and wristwatch into the canvas bag in one movement. He hadn't seen Seth's phone in his other hand. I breathed a two-second sigh of relief. Then Army Jacket was facing me.

Something strange happened then. Army Jacket just stood there, letting the moment drag on too long. He didn't say anything. He didn't take my watch or my wallet. He didn't even seem all that threatening. He was just . . . staring at me.

Did he know me? It was possible. Even though my brother

and I are supposed to be officially "retired," we'd put away a fair share of criminals in our time. Maybe this guy had been sent to prison, courtesy of Frank and Joe Hardy, and had just gotten his release.

See, our dad, Fenton Hardy, was once a world-famous detective. Growing up, Joe and I would help him on his cases. Then we began tackling mysteries on our own. We were proud of our successes. But after one too many close calls, things started to get a little out of hand, for reasons having to do with private investigators' licenses (we didn't have any), insurance (none of that, either), and the threat of being sued by every hoodlum we ever put under a citizen's arrest. Which is not how my brother and I wanted to spend the remainder of our teenage years, provided we're lucky enough to survive them. Some of us even have hopes of college one day . . . of a scholarship . . . of a normal life.

So with a few phone calls, including references from our principal and assurances to the police chief and state attorney general, we "retired." Officially, it stays that way—for all the Hardys. Our dad writes books on the history of law enforcement. And Joe and I go to high school.

That cozy arrangement, a.k.a. "the Deal," lasted about a month before Joe and I started going crazy. Maybe being a detective is something in your blood. I don't know.

Since then we've started taking the occasional case for a good cause or to help a friend, but we try to keep it confidential. And we deny everything. We don't consider it lying, just being prudent. We haven't told our dad, which makes me feel a bit guilty, but I get the feeling he suspects.

Not that it mattered right now. All that mattered was that Army Jacket's arm had slowly fallen to his side. His gun was pointed at the floor. Like he'd forgotten about it. Now was my chance.

I was about to grab the gun and wrestle it out of his hand, but his accomplice hollered, "Hey! What are you doing?"

Shocked back into the moment, Army Jacket raised his gun again. My chance was gone. I'd blown it. I could see the tiny mouth of the black barrel, aimed between my eyes. He was about to fire!

JOE

WAS STARING INTO A FACE I'D KNOWN MY ENTIRE life: my big brother Frank's. For a dizzy second or two, I forgot where I was and what I was doing.

It had totally slipped my mind that Frank had been sent on a phony errand down to the bank. Everybody in the Hardy family agreed he had been spending way too much time on the computer lately, and that he needed to go out and get some exercise and fresh air. The rain shower was just a bonus. Besides, Mom and Dad did all the household banking online. It is the twenty-first century, after all.

When I saw Frank, I almost blurted out his name. I caught myself just in time. But there had to be some way I could let him know it was me in the Michael Myers mask (the one from *Halloween*, you know). How could I signal to him? How could I let him know?

For a second, I thought about speaking to him in sign. Frank and I are both pretty fluent in American Sign Language. I could keep it simple: B-B G-U-N.

Letting him know, first of all, that I was just holding a BB gun. An unloaded one at that. It was the most important thing to communicate if we were going to stop these idiots!

But I'd better back up a little bit. You're probably wondering how Joe Hardy came to be holding up a bank in the company of two hardened criminals in the first place.

I had been on my way down to the Locker to meet Frank. (It's actually called the Meet Locker, which I think is kind of a stupid name. Most kids seem to agree and just call it the Locker.) Frank was all worked up about his speech, which was (as he had told me a million times) exactly one week away. Anyway, I was supposed to help him with it.

As I walked past the alley behind the bank, a big guy in a Michael Myers mask—just like the one I was wearing now—darted out from behind a car and yanked me off my feet. Now, before you call me a wuss, I do know judo (I'm a green belt). But the business end of a nine-millimeter Glock was pressed right up against my gut, so I played along.

It was not the first time I'd had a gun trained on me by some hoodlum. Frank and I had been solving crimes since we were little. We had to keep it on the down low nowadays, of course, because we kept getting sued. But the situation wasn't completely unfamiliar to me.

Mr. Glock dragged me over to a van. The door was wide open. Inside, a woman was squirming and whimpering, and when I took a closer look I recognized Mrs. Steigerwald, the owner of Bayport's bowling alley, Seaside Lanes. A big guy was holding another gun and had a hand clamped over her mouth, but he lifted it just long enough for her to shout, "Joe! Help m—"

She was wearing a baseball cap and these big, 1970s-style sunglasses—her usual getup—and she was so terrified, her glasses seemed to be fogging up. It was awful. The other gunman told me I had to help them rob the bank . . . or she'd "get it." Their partner hadn't shown up, he said, so they were a man short. Then the first guy tossed a big, greasy-looking army jacket at me and handed me another *Halloween* mask and the BB gun.

I racked my brain, but I couldn't see any way out. Poor Mrs. Steigerwald was about to hyperventilate.

"Don't worry, Mrs. S," I assured her, putting on the army jacket and the mask. "It'll all be over really quick. Then I'll come right out to check on you."

"All r-right . . . J-Joe," she answered through chattering teeth. Which surprised me, since she normally called everybody plain old "you." I didn't think she knew my name. I was always "You—the blond Hardy." But I let it slide, thinking she was just terrified.

Sixty seconds later, I was a felon.

Have you ever tried to hold up a bank with the sole aim of keeping anyone from being hurt? It's quite a high-wire act.

"Hey!" one of my accomplices barked at me now, snapping me back into the present. I'd been staring at Frank, trying to figure out how to communicate with him. "What are you doing?" he demanded.

There was no chance to team up with my brother at the moment. It was too risky. I just needed to get this ordeal over with as soon as possible. I took Frank's wallet and moved on.

The next customer in line brought me to a halt. This time I couldn't hide my shock.

"Um . . . Mrs. Steigerwald?" I said. My voice was muffled through the mask.

Mrs. Steigerwald looked freaked out—and mad. She wasn't wearing her hat and glasses now, and her bright-red hair stuck out at crazy angles. Her green eyes—a really memorable shade—stared at me suspiciously. She clutched her purse, getting ready to hit me with it. "What do you want, you?" she asked.

Now I was really confused. How was Mrs. Steigerwald standing right in front of me? If she was in the bank, who was out in the van being held captive? How could she be in two places at once?

"Were you just outside?" I asked her.

She looked confused. "When?"

"Like, two minutes ago."

"No," she replied. "I've been here for the past half hour, discussing Seaside Lanes's bank loan with Tom Baines." The color started returning to her cheeks as she got going. "Which I wouldn't need to do if the young people in this town would tear themselves away from their screens once in a while for some good, clean, healthy bowling!"

I took a deep breath, set my gun on the floor, and stepped away from it. Then I raised my hands over my head.

Frank nearly knocked the wind out of me when he tackled me and wrestled me to the ground. My brother looks skinny, but he has some power. I didn't resist. The bank erupted in chaos. People screamed. I caught a glimpse of the other two robbers ducking out the side door. The security guard ran over and put a knee in my back.

Frank ripped the mask off my face. To his credit, he didn't say anything. He just frowned.

"There's a really good explanation," I said.

"I bet there is," Frank answered.

Before I could get that explanation out, though, Bayport's finest were on the scene. Our town might have lousy cell phone reception, but I guess the landlines worked just fine.

I was in cuffs and out the door before I could say another word.